A VERY CRUMBLETON CHRISTMAS

CRUMBLETON BOOK 4

BETH RAIN

PROLOGUE

CRUMBLETON TIMES AND ECHO - 18TH DECEMBER

What's on This Week (we hope)

Christmas Lights Switch On. Date: TBC

It's going to happen, folks. This editor would like to apologise for the fact that we still don't have a firm date in the diary, what with the big day getting ever closer. After the storm forced us to cancel back in November, we're in desperate need of someone seriously sensational to do the honours and flip the switch.

Know a celeb? Contact Caroline today! (Really. Straight away. Don't dawdle!)

Film Review: Captain Woodentop Strikes Again

Does anyone need a good snooze? Then I recommend Jack Jones's latest thriller. Playing a secret agent on a mission to stop a rogue scientist, Jones's delivery has all the intensity of a casual Sunday stroll.

While explosions light up the screen and his co-stars do their best to bring the heat, Jones stumbles through the high-stakes chases with all the charisma of a coat rack.

Once again, Jack Jones exhibits less star-power than the trees in Crumbleton Clump, ensuring this potential pulse-pounding thriller flatlines with no chance of resuscitation.

Caroline Cook. Editor

CHAPTER 1

CAROLINE

'Aw come on Ruby… you know you want to!' wheedled Caroline, fluttering her eyelashes at her friend.

Ruby shook her head firmly and took a sip of tea as she settled further into the depths of the squashy sofa. She'd made a kind of writer's nest around herself, complete with laptop, blanket, and assorted notebooks.

The three friends were piled into the back room of Crumbleton Bookshop. It wasn't quite the setting Caroline had imagined when she'd called an emergency meeting… but Ruby had taken to writing on the giant sofa nestled between the bookshelves. It was practically impossible to get her to leave her perch when she was in the middle of a work in progress.

Golden lamplight reflected off the gilded spines of Oli's collection of antiquarian books surrounding them. The only sound other than their own chatter was the gentle tapping of Oli's laptop drifting through from the front of the shop. There were definitely worse places to hang out on a chilly, grey day a week before Christmas!

'Told you she wouldn't do it,' said Milly with a smirk from behind her own mug.

'But it's just the switch on of the Christmas lights,' said Caroline with a pout. 'It'll only take you two seconds… just a little speech and the flip of a switch. Look at it like this - it's your civic duty.'

'Nice try,' laughed Ruby, rolling her eyes, 'but you used that line last time you wanted me to cut a ribbon.'

'But you're my go-to celebrity!' said Caroline.

'I'm sure Milly wouldn't mind doing it for you,' said Ruby, unmoved. 'I mean, the switch *is* up at the museum – and her shop's literally two doors down!'

'Yeah… but I'm not a *celebrity author!*' said Milly with a grin.

'Me neither,' muttered Ruby.

'Nice try, Rubes,' said Milly, 'but considering you've got a film being made of your last book… you definitely are!'

'Well, it doesn't matter either way,' said Ruby with a shrug. 'I really can't. I'm sorry, but I've got this deadline.'

'So how come you've got time to drink tea with us, then?' said Caroline.

'Totally different,' said Ruby. 'This is professional procrastination. Besides, you said there was an emergency, and then you guys basically invaded my office.'

'She does have a point,' said Milly, stretching out in the comfy armchair, looking like she was thoroughly enjoying herself.

'I'm really sorry, Car,' said Ruby. 'But I've got until Christmas Eve to get this draft to my editor. She's already doing her nut in that I haven't sent her any chapters yet, so I'm going to be deep in the trenches this week. Even Oli's going to struggle to get a coherent sentence out of me until it's done!'

'Fairy snuff,' sighed Caroline.

'Anyway... I don't get it. Where's the emergency? Haven't the lights been on for a month already?' said Ruby.

'Yes... but we need to turn them off so that they can be *officially* turned back on,' said Caroline.

'Seriously?' said Ruby with a snort, raising an eyebrow at Milly as she started to giggle uncontrollably.

'It's important!' huffed Caroline. 'A tradition.'

'I'll take your word for it,' said Ruby. 'But if it's so important, how come you've left it so late to find someone?'

'You really do lose grip on reality when you're working on a book, don't you?' chuckled Milly.

'Maybe a bit,' said Ruby, looking surprised. 'Why?'

'Because I had a whole event planned for it back in

November,' said Caroline. 'Then we had that stupid storm, so I had to cancel it.'

'Then she got the flu,' said Milly, helping herself to a custard cream from the tin on the low table between them.

'Oh no – you poor thing,' said Ruby. 'I hope you're feeling better?'

'Four weeks later, I'm loads better, thanks,' said Caroline, shaking her head. 'Anyway, we need someone really good to turn the lights off and back on again before Boxing Day arrives and it's too late.'

'Couldn't you just... let it go?' said Milly gently. 'Just... let it pass by... just this once? I mean, it's not like Crumbleton's going to be deprived of their lights, is it?'

'Wash your mouth out,' said Caroline with an exaggerated huff. 'No way, not on my watch. I'd never live it down!'

'Okay, okay!' said Milly, holding her hands up in surrender. 'Right, if it's not going to be Rubes, who else can you ask?'

'How about the Cheswell Cup winner?' said Ruby. 'Kendra.'

'Already tried her,' said Caroline. 'She's gone away with her parents until New Year.'

'Shame,' said Milly. 'Erm... we could see if the mayor would do it?'

'No one's going to come to see the mayor!' chuckled Caroline. 'Bless her heart.'

'How about Cath?' said Ruby. 'Any money raised on the night is meant to benefit the museum, right?'

'It is,' said Caroline, 'but – as lovely as she is – I don't think Cath's quite the right person either.'

'Where is she this evening, anyway?' demanded Milly. 'Doesn't she know she's missing tea and very important gossip? Should I head upstairs and grab her?'

'Andy's taken her away for a few days,' said Caroline.

'Wait,' gasped Milly. 'Andy Morgan has actually stepped beyond Crumbleton's City Gates?'

'I know… it must be love!' said Caroline.

'Oh, it's definitely love,' said Ruby with a broad smile. 'Have you seen the pair of them together? It's like the entire world stops existing and…'

Ruby trailed off, her eyes glazing over. Then she snapped back into focus and grabbed one of her notebooks. Drawing the biro out from behind her ear, she started to scribble.

Caroline shot a wink over at Milly, and Milly grinned back. This was a regular occurrence when they got together and something sparked Ruby's imagination. The pair of them sat back and sipped their drinks in silence, waiting for her to re-emerge at the end of her thought.

Ten minutes later Ruby was still scribbling furiously in her little notebook, her pen a blur as she filled page after page. Caroline got to her feet and Milly followed suit. With whispered farewells, they made their way quietly through to the front of the shop.

'Hey!' said Oli in surprise, smiling at them from behind the till. 'You guys off already?'

'The muse has struck,' said Caroline with a tilt of her head towards the back room where Ruby was still hard at it.

'Mid-sentence, in fact,' added Milly.

'Finally!' said Oli, with a look of relief. 'Let's hope it sticks this time. I swear, I've never seen our flat this clean – she's been avoiding writing anything for days now.'

'And here I am, offering her the perfect excuse,' said Caroline, 'and she goes and turns me down!'

'Christmas lights?' said Oli.

Caroline nodded.

'She said no?' said Oli.

Caroline nodded again.

'Thank goodness!' said Oli. 'No offence, but at least it means she's serious about getting to the end of this draft.'

'We'd better go,' murmured Milly with a tiny nod towards the back room.

The three of them turned to peep at Ruby, only to find her glaring right back at them.

'We've officially entered writer-in-residence status!' whispered Oli. 'Run! Save yourselves!'

Caroline blew Ruby a kiss, and then she and Milly

shuffled out of the shop, giving Oli a tiny wave as they pulled the door closed behind them.

'You heading back up to the shop?' said Caroline.

'Nah,' said Milly, shaking her head. 'I've left Jo in charge for the rest of the afternoon. It's mostly just people picking up their Christmas wreaths today, so I'm going to spend the afternoon decorating the trawler.'

'Oh, nice,' said Caroline.

It wasn't her idea of fun, but after a whirlwind romance earlier in the year, Milly had moved in with Murray and now the pair of them lived on his giant trawler out in the middle of the marshes. It was strange what some people did for love.

'Shall I walk you down to the wharf, then?' said Caroline.

'I'm meeting Murray for lunch first down at the Dolphin and Anchor,' said Milly. 'Fancy joining us?'

Caroline shook her head. As much as she'd love to skive for the rest of the day, she had work to do.

'I'd better head back to the office and scan my contacts again.'

'Seriously?' said Milly.

'The event's not going to organise itself,' said Caroline.

'When is it, anyway?' said Milly as they set off down the hill together.

'Whatever night I can kidnap some random celeb and drag them to town!' said Caroline.

'Well, good luck with that,' said Milly.

'As long as the weather behaves itself...' said Caroline, eyeballing the dark grey duvet of cloud that had settled over Crumbleton and the marshes while they'd been in the bookshop.

'Erm, I don't think it's going to,' said Milly. 'Look!'

Caroline watched as her friend stuck out her hand. Sure enough – a soft white flake floated down to settle on her palm.

'I love Crumbleton at Christmas time,' she sighed.

'My first on the boat with Murray!' said Milly, with a broad smile.

'On that note, hadn't you better hurry?' said Caroline. 'Just in case this turns into proper snow.'

'Good thinking,' said Milly, pulling her in for a quick hug. 'Good luck on the celebrity hunt!'

Caroline waved as Milly trotted off, before following her down the hill at a much more leisurely pace. She wasn't in any kind of rush to go back to the office... but she really *did* need to find someone to switch the lights on.

❄

'Lee!' she said, in surprise.

The antique shop's large, slightly beaten-up van drew to a halt next to Caroline just as she reached the little courtyard in front of the Crumbleton Times and Echo offices.

'Hey Cazzzarooney!' said Lee, his grinning face appearing as he wound down the mud-splattered window.

'I thought that name had died out the minute we left secondary school,' huffed Caroline, wrapping her arms around herself. It felt like the temperature was plummeting, and she could swear the soft white flakes were already falling thicker and faster.

'You'll always be Cazzzarooney to me!' said Lee.

'Wonderful,' sighed Caroline. 'You'll always be an idiot to me!'

'Charming' laughed Lee.

Caroline grinned at him. They'd known each other since they'd been in nursery school, and Lee would never be anything other than the idiot who'd taken a pair of elephant safety scissors to her pigtails when she was six.

'Where's your nan?' said Caroline, wondering why Geraldine wasn't in her usual spot behind the wheel.

'She didn't fancy her chances getting up the high street later tonight if this weather gets any worse, so she's up at the shop and I'm doing the rounds early.'

'Good idea,' said Caroline.

'Actually, I've just been out delivering to Crumbleton Sands,' said Lee. 'That's why I stopped… I've got a bit of a scoop for you.'

'Oh yeah?' said Caroline, her ears pricking up.

'Yeah,' he said looking smug. 'You still trying to find someone to turn the Christmas lights on?'

Caroline nodded. She knew better than to get her hopes up, though – this was probably just the start of one of Lee's stupid jokes.

'Then I might have the perfect person for you,' he said.

'Oh yeah?' she said again, raising a sceptical eyebrow.

'Jack Jones.'

'Sod off,' chuckled Caroline.

'Hey – he'd be perfect!' said Lee.

'Yes... he would,' said Caroline, 'what with him being a massive Hollywood star and all.'

'Well,' said Lee, 'I just delivered a whopping set of bookshelves to that particular Hollywood star's house.'

'You're pulling my leg, right?' said Caroline.

'Hey, you're the one who broke the story about him buying a holiday home there,' said Lee. 'In fact, I seem to remember you went on a lovely long rant about it. *Unfair to the local community...* blah blah blah... *full-of-himself knob-head* ... blah blah blah!'

Caroline cringed. Yep. She'd said something along those lines. She'd also given his most recent film a less than favourable review. She'd called his performance wooden... and then she'd given him a lowly three stars.

Overcompensating much?!

The truth was, she had an enormous crush on Jack Jones. Always had – ever since his first walk-on part in the rom-com that had kick-started his career. The film had been awful, but that hadn't stopped her from falling head-over-fantasy for the dark-haired demi-god.

Caroline shifted her weight uncomfortably, suddenly glad that Lee wasn't a mind reader.

'Well... crap,' she muttered. 'That's not going to help my case much, is it?'

'I'd agree with you if there was any chance he'd actually read any of your rants,' said Lee, cocking his head, 'but let's face it – Jack Jones reading The Crumbleton Times and Echo? Not very likely, is it?!'

'You cheeky blighter,' huffed Caroline.

'I'm a truthful one, though,' said Lee with a broad grin. 'Besides, he'd be perfect for what you need, right? A genuine film star... even if you can't stand him.'

Caroline nodded. Lee was right – about the film star bit, at least.

'So...' she said, doing her best to sound nonchalant, 'what's the security like at his place? Cameras? Bodyguards?'

'Ah man, you're not going to break in and hold him hostage until he agrees, are you?' snorted Lee.

'No,' said Caroline, 'but I *am* going to go straight over there to ask him if he's up for it.'

'You're not serious?' said Lee, looking wary. 'Now?'

'Now,' said Caroline. She might as well strike while the iron was lukewarm.

'Leave it till tomorrow, Cazza,' said Lee, shaking his head. 'I know this snow doesn't look like much right now, but it's meant to get worse – and I swear I hit a slippery patch on the way across the marshes… even with all the salt in the air!'

'Aw cute – you're worried about me,' said Caroline with a cheeky smile. 'Don't worry, I'll go careful.'

'Fine,' said Lee, rolling his eyes. 'Don't say I didn't warn you, though.'

'Cheers for the tipoff!' said Caroline.

'Good luck,' said Lee. 'Be nice to him…'

'I'm always nice!' said Caroline.

'Uh-huh,' said Lee, raising an eyebrow. 'Poor bloke. Bye Cazzzarooney.'

Caroline watched as he disappeared off up the cobbles, and then stood for a long moment in the courtyard. Was she really going to do this?

Glancing up at the heavy clouds, Caroline rubbed her hands together, wishing she had her woolly gloves with her. Surely the snow wouldn't get too bad… she'd have time to nip over to Crumbleton Sands, wouldn't she? It shouldn't take long.

'Come on,' Caroline whispered to herself, her breath pluming in the chilly air. 'Let's go meet Jack Jones!'

CHAPTER 2

JACK

'Brian, my man, you're an absolute hero!' said Jack.

He heaved two laden carrier bags out of the boot of the taxi, while Brian hefted a box of groceries into his arms and followed Jack into the vast hallway of his seafront house.

'It's my pleasure,' said Brian, placing the heavy box down on a broad wooden bench and straightening up with a grin. 'Can't have a Hollywood star wandering around Bendall's... we'd have a riot on our hands!'

'Not sure about that,' Jack smirked, 'but I really do appreciate your help to keep my visits quiet.'

'I enjoy it,' said Brian. 'Mind you, it's a bit easier now that Trish is doing the housekeeping for you and knows what's going on.'

Jack grinned. Trish was Brian's wife and one of the sweetest women he'd ever met. Though, apparently she wasn't *quite* so sweet when she suspected her devoted husband was up to no good. It had taken a transatlantic video call before Trish would believe poor old Brian wasn't telling her some seriously tall tales.

'How is Trish?' he said.

'Perfect,' said Brian with a broad smile. 'She sends her love. Anyway, are you settling in okay? How's the jetlag this time?'

'You know how it is!' laughed Jack, shaking his head. 'I'm still half-living out of my suitcases, and my body clock is giving me the run-around... but I should be back on track in time for Christmas.'

'That's good,' said Brian. 'For the record, it's about time you had a proper break. I'm happy to bring you anything you need while you're here, if you want to keep a low profile... though the invitation still stands if you ever fancy a game of darts at the Dolphin and Anchor!'

'Cheers,' said Jack, 'but I think I'll be keeping myself to myself... at least for now.'

'Fair enough,' said Brian with a little shrug. 'Any idea how long you'll be staying?'

'I'm... undecided,' said Jack.

The truth was, he was knackered. He'd been on three back-to-back shoots, and the hectic press tour he'd just completed had nearly finished him off. Brian was right - he was desperate for a break.

'Sorry,' chuckled Brian. 'You don't have to tell me, I'm just being nosy.'

'Honestly, I'd be happy to tell you if I knew,' said Jack. 'I'd love nothing more than to take at least a month off – get the house sorted out at properly and start really turning it into a home...'

'Sounds like a good plan to me,' said Brian with an approving nod.

'Problem is, my agent keeps saying things like *"we need to ride this wave!"* sighed Jack. 'The woman's relentless! She doesn't care that it's nearly Christmas... or that I've taken myself offline for a break.'

'At least she can't get at you quite so easily while you're here,' said Brian. 'She's in LA, right?'

'Yep,' said Jack. 'Unfortunately, the minute Aimee realised I wasn't checking my emails, she started sending me blasted scripts in the post. There was a whole box waiting for me when I arrived... and three more came this morning!'

'Well, it's not all bad,' said Brian. 'At least it means we'll be treated to another Jack Jones movie soon.'

'Maybe,' said Jack.

'Maybe?' gasped Brian. 'Don't tease me!'

Jack shrugged. There wasn't much he could say. Until the right script came along, he had nothing else in the works. That was probably why Aimee was being quite so persistent. He was the current talk of the town... but all he really wanted was a bit of peace and quiet. He loved his work, but everything that went with it could be... overwhelming.

'Here,' said Jack, deciding to change the subject. He

handed Brian the envelope of cash he had waiting for him. He'd tucked a hefty Christmas tip in there along with both Trish and Brian's fees and the cost of his groceries.

'Cheers!' said Brian, tucking the envelope away without looking inside.

'No – thank you!' said Jack, eyeballing the goodies Brian had picked up for him. 'This little lot should see me through until Boxing Day. I don't know what I'd do without you!'

'Well... if you need anything else, just give me a shout,' said Brian. 'Happy to help – and Trish said the same.'

'Give her a Christmas hug for me when you get home?' said Jack.

'That'll make her year,' said Brian with a grin. 'In fact, I'm going to head home now. I don't like the look of those clouds – it was already starting to snow when I left town!'

'Well, safe drive, my man,' said Jack, clapping him on the shoulder. 'Merry Christmas.'

'You too,' said Brian, ambling back towards the taxi and hopping in. Just as he was about to pull away, he rolled his window down and gave Jack a fatherly glare. 'I meant to say – stay out of the sea!'

'You know I can't promise you that,' said Jack.

Brian had been like a stuck record about Jack's cold water swimming habit ever since he'd discovered his addiction to jumping the garden fence and legging it down the beach into the waves.

'Well, at least promise me you'll wear a bright hat if you're idiot enough to go in?' said Brian. 'I don't want to be reading about a celebrity cold-water-swimming tragedy in the newspaper next week!'

'Don't worry – there's not much chance of that. I don't think the reporter at the Crumbleton Times would see it as much of a tragedy,' said Jack, rolling his eyes. 'She doesn't like me very much.'

'Caroline Cook's bark is worse than her bite,' said Brian with an amused grin. 'That woman is a big pussy cat when you get to know her.'

'Pussy cats scratch,' said Jack. 'Plus, they hiss and spit.'

'I don't know why you insist on me sending you a copy of the newspaper every week,' chuckled Brian.

'Because it's best to know what the enemy's saying about you!' said Jack said with a raised eyebrow.

In reality, he rather enjoyed reading the local news... even when he was on the other side of the world. It made him feel connected to home. Plus – he loved Caroline Cook's writing – not that he'd ever admit it, of course. She was sharp and incredibly funny. Her review of his last film had reduced him to tears of laughter, and he'd cut it out and popped it into a frame for his dressing room. She might not be very keen on him, but he was most definitely a fan of hers!

'Anyway,' said Jack, shaking his head, 'since I don't

want to give Caroline Cook the satisfaction of reporting on my premature demise – I promise to wear a bright hat. I've got a swim float too.'

'Good,' said Brian. 'Right, I'd best be off before those clouds decide to take themselves a bit more seriously.'

Even as Jack raised his hand to wave Brian off, a couple of white flakes drifted lazily onto the driveway. Jack smiled at the sight of them. He loved snow, and Brian should be nice and safe at home before this little flurry they were in for had the chance to settle – which was a relief.

The man was a saint. There weren't many people Jack trusted to keep his whereabouts quiet, but frankly, he'd trust Brian with his life. Trish too, come to that. Jack liked the fact that the pair of them treated him as a regular person – just Jack who was brought up less than twenty miles along the coast. Just Jack – who might fancy a festive game of darts over a pint. Just Jack – not some trumped-up Hollywood star in hiding.

With a huge sigh, Jack pushed the front door closed and started to carry his groceries through to the kitchen. It was probably his favourite room in the whole house – mainly because it had the best view of the sea.

Jack had bought his dream house in Crumbleton Sands a couple of years ago, but so far, he'd not really been able to spend as much time there as he'd hoped.

'At least you're here for Christmas!' he said, starting to stash goodies away in random cupboards before turning to the fridge. This little lot should mean he could survive right the way through until Boxing Day without having to leave the house if he didn't want to.

As soon as the fridge was groaning with enough cold meat, olives, cheese and assorted nibbles to feed a small country, Jack made his way over to the floor-to-ceiling windows that looked straight out across the golden dunes that separated his house from the sea.

The low-hanging clouds had turned the waves into a deep, moody blue beyond the lacy curtain of the snowflakes as they drifted around aimlessly. It was just coming up to high tide, so there was only a narrow fringe of sandy beach visible above the lapping waves.

The sight made him long for a swim.

Why not?

'Because it's snowing – idiot!' he answered himself. Then he shrugged. Why should he let that stop him?!

A swim might help nudge his jetlag back a bit… and maybe calm his racing thoughts too. As much as he was here to relax and unwind, he was having a hard time switching off. The cold water would help. It always did.

He had his wetsuit laid out upstairs… he'd treat himself to a quick dip, and then settle in and make a dent in some of the goodies Brian had just delivered.

Pausing for just a few more seconds, Jack watched the snowflakes dip and swirl as they drifted down to meet the sea. The sight made his heart squeeze with pure joy. This was exactly why he'd fallen in love with this house in the first place. He had unrestricted views across the sea at the back of the house, and he didn't even need to leave his own garden to get down onto the beach... he could just hop the fence and then make a dash straight across the dunes and into the sea.

'Sorry Brian, I'm going in!' said Jack, spinning on his heel and dashing upstairs to get changed.

Darting into his vast bedroom, Jack made a beeline for his wetsuit which he'd laid out on the ottoman at the foot of the bed. He had to pick through the piles of scripts lying all over the floor to get to it. Poor Trish – she'd have a fit if she could see what a mess he'd made of the pristine house in the few days he'd been back.

Jack had ordered a bookshelf from Crumbleton Antiques so that he could get himself a bit more organised, and it had arrived about an hour ago. He *really* needed to sort this lot out – before he managed to break an ankle – or worse! But... the scripts could stay put for a little while longer, couldn't they?!

'First things first!'

Jack started to strip off his clothes. Stepping out of his jeans he couldn't help but laugh at his deep Californian tan. It wasn't going to do him much good here. As much as he looked like the picture of health in a pair of board shorts while splashing around in a pool or the Pacific Ocean, it would be thoroughly covered up when he dived into the waves here.

A nice, warm wetsuit, along with a pair of boots and neoprene gloves to stop his fingers turning blue the minute he got into the water were most definitely the order of the day when it came to December swims in Crumbleton Sands!

As he started the arduous task of squeezing himself into his tadpole suite, Jack eyeballed the hat he'd laid out next to it. Dark blue with a bobble. It was certainly warm, but he'd promised Brian he'd go bright.

'Erm... let me see,' he muttered, glancing around his tip of a bedroom while he tugged the wetsuit further up his legs. His eyes came to rest on the latest pile of scripts that had arrived in the post that morning. He hadn't even looked through them yet – the sight of them had just made him want to curl up in a ball and sleep until New Year.

Jack had left them in a heap on the carpet, along with the packaging and the Christmas card and joke gift Aimee had included.

'Perfect!' said Jack, eyeballing the bright red and white furry Santa hat she'd sent him – along with strict instructions not to get caught wearing it in public.

Jack shrugged. It wasn't very likely anyone would spot him enjoying a Christmas dip in Crumbleton Sands! If they did... well... it was on her for sending it to him in the first place!

Grabbing the hat from the pile, he yanked it onto his head with a grin. It was time for this Santa to swim!

Heading downstairs, Jack left the front door on the latch behind him. The last thing he wanted to do was lock himself out. He could only imagine what a locksmith would say – faced with a call-out from a wetsuit-wearing film star in a Santa hat!

Striding through the swirling snowflakes, Jack made his way around the back of the house and through the garden. Then hopped over the low bit of fence and jogged up and over the dunes that separated his property from the sea.

The sound of the crashing waves sent a buzz of energy coursing through his body, and Jack let out an excited howl as he ran towards the water... low at first but then louder and louder as he neared the sea.

Jack loved every trip to the beach. It didn't matter that he was down there two or three times some days, every single visit was like a reset for his soul. Today felt even more magical than usual as soft flakes drifted around him and the waiting waves beckoned him forwards. There wasn't another soul in sight - the sands were completely deserted.

Jack had never been one of those slow waders – and he set off at a gallop, darting towards the cold water – the white pompom of his Santa hat dancing merrily as he went.

'Wheeeeeee!' Jack's voice came out a high-pitched cry of delight as the first hit of ice-cold salt water made its way through the fabric of his swim shoes. Two seconds later, he dove into the waves, head-first.

Spluttering and as he surfaced, Jack realised that had been a rookie move... his hat had washed clean off his head.

Giggling to himself, he swam after it as it drifted just out of reach and pulled the drenched material onto his head. Splashing around like a lunatic, Jack lifted his face to the sky and howled in pure delight as snowflakes kissed his cheeks.

There was no way he'd be able to do this in California – for one thing, he'd not be able to make it down the beach without having to stop for a billion selfies before he even reached the water. For another, there was always paparazzi… and he was pretty sure that Aimee wouldn't be too pleased about a bunch of photos of him behaving like a toddler.

'Woohooo!' he cheered, just for good measure, before striking out across the bay as the snow swirled overhead.

CHAPTER 3

CAROLINE

It was just as well Caroline knew the road to Crumbleton Sands like the back of her hand. She was only halfway there when the snow stopped messing around and started to fall in earnest. It was now swirling around the car like it was on a mission to confuse her, and she was thoroughly regretting her rash decision to turn up on Jack Jones's doorstep unannounced... mostly because she wasn't entirely sure she'd actually get there.

'Lee did warn you,' she muttered, gripping her steering wheel as she leaned so far forward in her seat that she practically had her nose pressed against the windscreen. Unfortunately, it didn't do much to help her see through the drifting snow.

Caroline's mum had always said that her stubbornness would get her into trouble one day. Somehow, she had a feeling this might just be that day!

If she'd thought for a moment that the weather would turn this bad so fast, she wouldn't have set off in the first place.

Probably.

'Since when did Lee start talking sense?' she huffed. The day she started taking that idiot seriously was the day hell froze over.

Caroline winced.

Poor choice of words there!

This might not be hell, but it was definitely starting to freeze over!

She flipped her windscreen wipers up to triple speed and strained her eyes as she crept across the junction that would lead her towards Crumbleton Sands. With any luck, the closer she got to the sea, the calmer the snowstorm would be.

Ten minutes later, Caroline's knuckles had turned white. Still, she'd managed to make it safely across the marshes and was now crawling along the coast road towards the property Jack Jones had bought as his holiday home.

Caroline had never seen snow like this so close to the coast before. As treacherous as it was driving through the swirling flakes, she couldn't stop herself from taking regular peeks across the dunes towards the sea. It was absolutely stunning and completely deserted.

Wait... maybe not completely...

'Is that someone… swimming?!' she gasped.

Her eyes had just snagged on two spots of colour cutting through the grumpy-looking waves. It looked like someone was out there with a swim float and... a Santa hat?!

'What a nutter!'

Caroline shivered and quickly focussed back on the road. She had enough to worry about without landing the car in a ditch just because she was watching someone brave the waves in the snow!

Now that she was almost at her destination, Caroline's stomach was busy reminding her that she was about to do something spectacularly silly. She hadn't considered what she'd actually do when she got to Jack Jones's house. Would there be a security guard? Gates? Maybe there'd be one of those intercom things where she had to announce her arrival and wait for one of Jack's lackeys to buzz her inside.

'Might as well face it... I'm doomed,' sighed Caroline, wishing she'd managed to extract more information out of Lee before she'd dashed off on this fool's errand.

No celeb in their right mind would let some random visitor wander into their home after turning up unannounced – let alone a member of the press.

Maybe she could do a bit of a drive-by first. That would give her the chance to figure out the lay of the land and make a plan. Of course, it *might* be a good idea to leave her car elsewhere and walk the rest of the way to the house - but considering the sky was thick with snowflakes and the road was getting more slippery by the second, she really wasn't up for that!

As she approached the stunning seaside property, Caroline slowed down even further so that she could have a good look. From what she could remember, the house had a vast front gate – an imposing metal affair with spikes along the top…

'Okay, I wasn't expecting that!' she gasped.

The gate stood wide open. If she was brave enough, there was nothing to stop her from pulling right into the driveway.

'No point chickening out now!' she muttered.

Yanking at the indicator stalk, Caroline pulled through the open gateway before she could change her mind.

She was about to knock on Jack Jones's front door. *The* Jack Jones. The one she'd had a crush on ever since she'd watched that first awful flop of a film. Jack Jones, who she'd basically torn limb from limb in the paper on a number of occasions.

Get a grip, woman. It'll be fine – there's no way he'll know about that!

Drawing the car to a stop on the paved driveway, Caroline killed the engine. Then she took a deep breath and clambered out before her nerve deserted her.

The driveway was already turning slick with snowflakes as they started to settle, and Caroline sent up a little prayer of thanks that she was wearing flats. Moving gingerly towards the glossy red front door,

Caroline took another deep breath as she peered around for an intercom to announce her arrival… or a camera… or *anything* high-tech.

'Really… just a doorbell?' she whispered. 'Well, here goes nothing.'

Reaching out a shaking finger, she pressed hard on the metal button and then strained her ears.

Nothing.

No resulting trill of a bell deep inside the house. No footsteps. Nada. Just the not-so-distant sound of the waves crashing against the shore.

Caroline frowned. Perhaps the bell wasn't working. Maybe she should just call it quits and leave?

'Maybe not!' she muttered, her signature stubborn streak rising to the surface.

Reaching out again, she rapped hard on the shiny red paint, tapping out a jaunty little beat. Then she cringed. What a great first impression to give a film star!

After listening intently for several long seconds, Caroline let out a disappointed sigh. There were still no signs of life from inside. Either Jack Jones wasn't in, he'd spotted her pulling up and was currently hiding as though his life depended on it, or Lee had been pulling her leg and the man wasn't even in the country – let alone this house! The third option seemed to be the most likely – especially considering the gate had been left open.

If Lee had been messing with her and she'd risked

her neck on the slippery roads for nothing, she was going to wring *his* neck... but then... there *were* lights on inside.

Caroline hammered on the front door again, not being quite so demure and cutesy about the whole thing this time around.

Still no answer.

Well, she clearly wasn't going to get to meet Jack Jones today... but maybe she could sneak a peek inside while she was here.

Turning her back on the front door, Caroline crunched her way along the narrow strip of honey-coloured gravel that ran around the house. She made her way towards the enticing beam of golden light that spilled through one of the ground-floor windows.

Cupping her hands against the glass, Caroline was just about to have a good look inside when the sound of swift footsteps made her jump back as though the house had just smacked her in the face.

Only just in time, too!

A figure came jogging around the corner, wearing a wetsuit and a sodden Santa hat.

'Hi!' she squeaked.

She definitely had resting-guilt-face right now.

The man came to an abrupt halt. He blinked at her a few times – maybe in surprise, or possibly because salt water was dripping from the Santa hat straight into his eyes.

'Hi!' he said – frozen to the spot.

Was she hallucinating right now, or was she staring at Jack Jones? *The* Jack Jones... film star... mega-crush. Caroline cleared her throat, doing her best to keep her eyes on his face. It was a *very* revealing wetsuit!

'Hi!' she said again, this time her voice a faint tremor.

'You'd better come in.'

If she hadn't actually seen his slightly blue lips moving, Caroline would have thought the words were just a figment of her imagination.

'In?' she murmured.

Jack Jones simply gave her a broad, slightly mad-looking grin as he headed straight past her towards the front door, the white pompom on his hat dripping as he went.

'Make yourself at home,' he called over his shoulder as he disappeared inside. 'I'll be with you in just a sec.'

Caroline blinked. This couldn't be happening... maybe she'd slipped on the snow and banged her head? She gave the back of her hand a sharp pinch.

'Ouch!'

Okay, so this was real, then? Jack Jones had just appeared in a wetsuit and invited her into his home without even knowing who she was?

Weird... but... okay!

Turning and getting a face full of snowflakes in the process, Caroline shook her head and hurried towards the front door before Jack Jones could come to his senses and change his mind.

The man in question was nowhere to be seen – the only sign of him was a trail of wet footprints leading inside – so Caroline stepped into the blissfully warm hallway and closed the door behind her. The sound was echoed by another door slamming somewhere overhead.

'Okay, wow,' said Caroline, shaking the snow from her hair and staring around the vast entrance hall.

The floor was a mosaic of colourful tiles, an old-fashioned glass lampshade hung overhead, and the staircase swept up to the first floor in a glossy wooden curve. The house had an air of grandeur about it, but not in the way she might have expected. It was more old-school charm than LA designer chic. There were a couple of slightly tatty rugs on the tiles, and a sturdy wooden bench sat against one wall. There were a couple of empty cardboard boxes piled beneath it, along with a pair of discarded Wellington boots.

Caroline was surprised. The place somehow felt more like a family home than the fancy-pants holiday pad of a movie star. She desperately wanted to have a look around the rest of the place to see if the other rooms were the same… but she really *should* wait here, shouldn't she?

'He said make yourself at home!' she muttered.

But no… he'd probably just meant she was welcome to perch on the wooden bench so that she was out of the snow.

Probably!

Caroline shrugged. Someone was bound to be watching her every move on a hidden security camera. If she wandered somewhere she wasn't supposed to, she was sure they'd turn up and put her straight. Besides, she was a reporter... it was practically her duty to snoop!

Before she could talk herself out of it, Caroline crept to the far end of the hallway. To the right, she could just make out signs of a kitchen through a panelled glass door – a *very* expensive-looking coffee machine sat on the far side of a slate-topped island.

Hmm... maybe not! There had to be somewhere more interesting to have a nosey around than the kitchen!

'How about in here?!' she whispered, choosing the nearest heavy wooden door. Keeping her fingers crossed that she wasn't about to walk in on a bunch of security guards watching her every move on a bank of monitors, she turned the handle and pushed her way inside.

Phew!

There wasn't a security guard in sight.

'Gorgeous!' breathed Caroline, as a wave of warmth from a vast fireplace washed over her.

Jack Jones's living room exuded an aura of cosiness, and sure enough, it didn't give off designer-holiday-home vibes either. It had a high ceiling, complete with a beautiful plaster rose. Warm light bloomed from multiple vintage glass shades and twinkled off a handful of baubles that dangled from the branches of a humongous Christmas tree on the far side of the room.

The tree stretched all the way to the ceiling, and its scent hung heavy in the air. Judging by the open cardboard box on the floor next to it - and the fact that about eighty per cent of the tree's branches were still bare – Jack Jones must have only just started to decorate it.

'Or one of his staff, more likely!' she murmured.

Near the tree, standing at an awkward angle away from the walls, was a familiar-looking, empty bookshelf. She recognised the heavy piece of furniture from the back room of Geraldine's antique shop. So – Lee hadn't been pulling her leg after all!

Caroline shivered. The few minutes she'd spent pottering around outside had left her chilled to the bone, though she had a feeling the shivering had more to do with getting an eyeful of a certain movie star in a seriously clingy wetsuit!

Wrapping her arms around herself, she shot a longing look at the handsome wood burner set inside the immense stone fireplace. Sidling over to it, she turned her back to the flickering flames and started to toast her bum.

She shivered again. To think – somewhere above her head, Jack Jones was having a shower!

As though in answer to the thought, the distant sound of a rich baritone singing a Christmas song reached her ears. Someone was clearly enjoying their shower! Caroline grinned as her brain began to work on catchy headlines for a tell-all exposé...

Spotted! Hollywood Hunk Dons Wetsuit for Christmas Dip - Caught Crooning Carols in Shower Serenade!

Breaking: Star Caught in Wet and Wild Christmas Swim – Shower Carols Included!

Caroline giggled and shook her head.
'Stop it!'
She wasn't about to start gathering snippets for an all-access story... no matter how much her journalistic senses were tingling with potential. That sort of thing really wasn't her style. Besides, for whatever reason, the man had trusted her enough to let her into his house. It was only fair to return the favour by being a model guest. She'd simply sit and wait for him to reappear.

Caroline glanced at the collection of cosy sofas gathered around the fireplace, all three of them angled to make the most of its warmth. They weren't in the best shape – and one of them looked decidedly worn. There was even a small tear on the armrest, barely covered by a fleecy tartan blanket.

Well... she had three to choose from and there was no one around to watch... so she might as well give them all a trial run!

Bouncing down onto the nearest one, Caroline

snuggled into the corner. Not bad – but it was a bit too spongy for her taste. She scrabbled to her feet again and made for the deep-blue monster directly opposite the fireplace. This sofa was absolutely vast – and would probably make an excellent spot for an afternoon nap. In fact, the sight of it was making her more than a bit jealous. Her own settee was a tiny two-seater, and it was impossible to stretch out on it properly. She always ended up with a cricked neck or a dead leg after nodding off on it.

'Still not quite right,' she murmured from her prone position. It might be vast, but it needed more cushions to burrow into.

Hauling herself back to her feet, Caroline dived onto the third and final sofa. It might be the most threadbare of the lot – complete with that little rip, but...

'Perfect!'

Grinning at the fact that she'd basically just turned into the Goldilocks of sofas, Caroline ran her palms over the worn cotton covers and let out a contented little sigh. She'd be happy to spend her entire life in this spot. It was the perfect distance from the wood burner – not too warm, not too cool, and she could see the dancing flames through the little glass windows. But it wasn't just that which made this her top sofa pick - she also had an unrestricted view of the sea through the windows on the opposite side of the room.

Fire and waves all in one view? Count her in!

With another happy little sigh, Caroline slipped off her shoes and tucked her feet up underneath her as she snuggled back into the cushions.

'Comfy?!'

Caroline whipped around, only to find Jack Jones staring at her from the doorway.

CHAPTER 4

JACK

Jack had been standing there for several long moments, watching as his unexpected guest settled into his sofa.

His *favourite* sofa.

He'd had to bite his lip to stop himself from laughing when she'd stared lovingly at the fire and let out a happy little sigh. When she'd turned to glance out of the window at the swirling snowflakes and crashing waves beyond, he could swear she was about to pass out from a joy overload. Not that he could blame her, of course… the view had the same effect on him.

When she'd slipped her shoes off and tucked her feet up underneath her, Jack hadn't been able to hold back his snort of laughter any longer. It was a bit of a shame, as the peaceful tableau had ended abruptly.

Caroline Cook snapped to attention. The look of mortification on her pretty face left him caught somewhere between wanting to giggle and wanting to know how *anyone* could be quite so cheeky.

'When I said *make yourself comfortable*, it was only a figure of speech!' he said, his voice coming out all huffy and indignant, even though he was having a seriously hard time keeping a smile off his face.

Caroline promptly attempted to jump to her feet, stumbled on her discarded shoes, and toppled straight back into the cushions.

That did it. Jack let out a loud, surprised roar of laughter and received a deliciously red-faced, sheepish grin in return.

'That's my favourite sofa, too,' he said. Then, with great effort, he straightened his face again and even managed a little frown. 'Anyway – follow me!'

Jack turned and padded off towards the kitchen. He could hear his visitor struggling up out of the cushions again, though judging by the lighter-than-air footsteps that followed him two seconds later, she hadn't bothered to put her shoes back on.

'You know you're leaving wet footprints, right?' came a small voice.

'Don't worry,' Jack shrugged, 'the house is used to it!'

It was true – he was always tracking in sand and saltwater from the beach – much to Trish's consternation. This time, though, it was clean water from the shower for a change. Jack hadn't taken long to get out... not compared to his usual hour-long soaks, anyway! He'd was too curious to know what Caroline Cook was doing on his doorstep. On top of that, a small voice at the back of his head kept pointing out that it might *not* be the best idea to let a reporter roam around the house completely unsupervised.

After a quick rub-down with his towel, he'd thrown on a pair of ancient jeans and a tatty tee-shirt and dashed back downstairs. Maybe he should have taken a bit more care with his appearance considering he had a guest, but he *was* off duty. Besides, she'd invited herself over - so she'd just have to put up with him as he was.

'So,' said Jack, rounding the large slate kitchen island and facing her still slightly pink face across its expanse.

'Erm... yeah,' she said, staring at him.

He had to hand it to her, she was making impressive eye contact, given the circumstances.

'You're probably wondering who I am,' she added.

'Not really,' said Jack.

'Huh?'

'I already know who you are!' said Jack. Again, he had to bite back a smile at the look of pure surprise that crossed her face. 'You're Caroline Cook, editor of the Crumbleton Times and Echo.'

'I... I... how?' said Caroline.

'Come on... you didn't think I'd let a complete stranger into my house while I was having a shower, did you?' said Jack.

'But... I,' Caroline paused and shook her head. 'But we *are* strangers!'

'Not really,' said Jack.

'We've not met before!' said Caroline.

'Well, no,' said Jack, 'but I *do* know for a fact that you're not an over-eager, crazed fan who's going to run off with my underwear the minute I turn my back!'

Caroline let out a little splutter. 'Well no... I guess you would think that.'

Jack watched with interest as she started to fidget. He was having a seriously hard time keeping a straight face, but he didn't feel like letting her off the hook too soon.

Caroline broke eye contact and started to stare around the room as though she was looking for an escape route. Her eyes landed on his awards - dotted onto the same shelf as the tea and coffee – all woven together with a string of tinsel.

'Very festive,' she said, raising an eyebrow.

'Mmm,' he said. It was impossible to get a read on the woman. She was a strange mixture of supremely cheeky, horribly guilty and ridiculously funny. 'So... I suppose you're going to splash my name all over the front page of the paper next week?'

'Nope,' said Caroline, snapping back to look at him. 'Actually, I came to ask you for a favour.'

Jack's eyebrows flew up. Of all the things he'd been expecting – from stuttering excuses to bold-faced interview questions – a favour hadn't even crossed his mind.

'Oh?' he said lightly, as though she hadn't just completely thrown him for a loop.

'I was hoping you might be up for turning on Crumbleton's Christmas lights?'

'Isn't it a bit late for that?' said Jack. 'Christmas *is* in a week, right? Or have I fallen into some kind of weird vortex?'

'I've had a few problems finding a special guest,' huffed Caroline.

'Well... I'm not sure I'm all that special,' said Jack, folding his arms over his chest and holding her gaze. 'I mean, I thought you found my last performance... how did you put it again...? Ah, I remember - *"So wooden the trees in Crumbleton Clump have more star-quality."*'

'I... you... I...' spluttered Caroline, the look of mortification firmly back on her face.

'And then you gave me three stars,' said Jack, fighting back a bubble of laughter, 'for the fact that I spoke passable English.'

'You... you...'

Jack's grin finally broke through his stony façade, but going by the look on his guest's face, it didn't do anything to ease her horror that he really did know *exactly* who she was and what she'd written about him.

'Yep,' he said, unable to contain his glee, 'I'm afraid I'm intimately acquainted with your writing.'

'Oh,' said Caroline, turning away from him. 'Shit.'

Jack sniggered.

'I'm sorry to intrude,' said Caroline, throwing him an apologetic look. 'I should go.'

'Wait!' said Jack quickly. 'Now that I've got you here, I'd love to know what you think of my *"ostentatious holiday home."* What was it you said...? *"It'll be empty fifty weeks of the year, and things will only be worse when the rich nincompoop is in residence."*

Caroline's eyes widened, and she nodded slowly.

'Nincompoop,' she whispered, echoing him. 'I... I did say that.'

'So,' said Jack, deciding it was finally time to give her a break, 'what do you fancy - tea or coffee?'

Caroline went completely still, and then a broad, beautiful smile spread across her face. At last, it looked like she'd cottoned on. Far from being upset about what she'd written - Jack was just enjoying winding her up.

'You, Jack Jones,' she muttered, 'are a git.'

'Better than nincompoop,' chuckled Jack, reaching for two gigantic mugs with dancing gingerbread men painted on the front. 'And for the record, it's just Jack. You don't need to keep using my full name!'

'But that's just... weird,' she said.

'Excuse me?' said Jack.

'It's like calling Ryan Reynolds... well... Ryan!' said Caroline. 'It's just wrong!

'But that's his name,' laughed Jack.

'You're a movie star,' she huffed, 'of course you wouldn't get it!'

Jack raised an eyebrow and promptly decided not to mention the fact that he'd almost peed himself with excitement when he'd met Ryan Reynolds for the first time.

Ryan. Just Ryan!

'Actually... I kinda get where you're coming from,' he said. 'But as I'm off-duty, and you're in my house... can I be just Jack?'

Caroline cocked her head. 'Okie dokie, just Jack, I'll do my best.'

'Cheers!' he said. 'Now... what do you want to drink?'

'Coffee, please,' she said. 'Mainly because I want to see if you have to call a maid or something to get that beast of a machine to work!'

'You seriously think I have a maid hiding around here somewhere?' he laughed.

'And a whole room full of security guards,' said Caroline. 'I mean, why else would you let me in?!'

'Good question,' said Jack. 'Maybe I shouldn't admit to this... but just for the record – there's no one else here.'

'Really?' said Caroline, raising a sceptical eyebrow.

'Yep – just me on my lonesome,' said Jack. 'I come here when I need some peace and quiet... and when I need to get away from the press.'

'Oops, my bad,' said Caroline.

Jack shrugged. 'You don't count.'

'Jeez, thanks!' she said with a smirk and an extravagant eye roll.

'I didn't mean it like that,' said Jack quickly. 'You've got more writing talent in your little finger than most of the reporters I've had to deal with.'

'I… oh!' said Caroline, her cheeks turning pink again. 'Well… thanks.'

'I'm serious,' said Jack, turning to the coffee machine and firing up the grinder before meeting her eye again. 'What I meant was – you don't appear to have a long-lens stashed up your jumper.'

'Well, that's true at least!' said Caroline. 'I guess now might be a good time to apologise for being so mean in my reviews. I shouldn't have—'

'Stop,' chuckled Jack. 'They were hilarious, even if my ego took a bit of a battering. And just for the record – I do get the concern about me owning a house here – leaving it empty when I'm working and bringing unwanted attention when I *am* here.'

Caroline looked both intrigued and mildly uncomfortable. 'I really *am* sorry I wrote that. You can buy property wherever you fancy – it's got nothing to do with me.'

'You're a reporter,' said Jack with a shrug, turning back towards the coffee machine. 'Everything's to do with you. But the real story here is that this is my home – my one-and-only. I don't own anywhere else.

Filming drags me all over the place, but there's nowhere I'd rather be than here.'

'Well... I...' Caroline paused. 'I can see why,' she said eventually.

'Right?' said Jack. 'That view!'

Caroline followed his gaze through the window, and they both went quiet for a long moment.

'I have to say, it's nice to be sleeping in my own bed for a change,' said Jack, 'instead of some random hotel or a trailer on set.'

'So glamorous!' said Caroline with a little sigh.

'It's really not, you know,' said Jack.

He knew he probably sounded like a spoiled git enjoying a pity party, but the reality of shooting on location wasn't nearly as glamorous or exciting as everyone seemed to think.

'It's long days, uncomfortable nights, and hour after boring hour spent in makeup. Then – after months of living in a weird little bubble – you get dumped into a room full of press where you're expected to sound halfway human.'

'Hmm,' said Caroline. 'I guess I never thought about it like that. Sounds... chaotic?'

'That's a good word for it,' said Jack. 'I mean, I love the acting part of it all but... let's just say I've been looking forward to coming home for some peace and quiet. Now here I am, and the press are all over me again!'

Jack winked at Caroline, but she looked more than a little bit guilty.

'Sorry,' she muttered.

'Don't be!' said Jack. 'I'm just pulling your leg. You might not be a fan of my work, but—'

'Hey Jack?' said Caroline, cutting straight across him.

It was probably a good thing, as he'd been about to make a total goofball of himself by telling her outright that he was a fan of *her* work. How cringey could he get?!

'Yeah?'

'Do you think we can start over?' she said. 'Would you mind pretending you never read any of those stupid things I wrote about you?'

'Hm...,' said Jack. 'As you asked so nicely, I guess we could do that. It's Christmas, after all, right?'

'Right,' said Caroline, the relief evident in her voice.

'While we're apologising for things,' said Jack, shifting a stack of scripts out of the way so that he could place her cup of coffee in front of her, 'sorry about the state of the place. I wasn't expecting guests! I've not been back long and, to be honest, I'm still getting over the jetlag.'

'Is that what the mad cold-water swimming is about?' said Caroline, sipping her coffee and letting out a contented little sigh that, for some reason, did something strange to Jack's stomach.

'Swimming? I mean... yeah, it does help,' he said,

'but I just love it. I'm in and out of the water all the time when I'm here.'

'Weirdo,' said Caroline.

'I'll take that as a compliment,' said Jack.

'You definitely should!' said Caroline.

'So,' said Jack, sliding into a seat opposite her and raising his mug, 'here's to unexpected guests.'

Caroline mirrored him.

'Now,' he said, 'tell me more about this Christmas lights thing!'

CHAPTER 5

CAROLINE

'Oh!' said Caroline, staring at Jack in surprise. She hadn't been expecting him to voluntarily bring the subject back around to her supremely cheeky request so soon! 'Sure, what do you want to know?'

'Well… what would I have to do?' he said before sipping his coffee with obvious relish.

'It's not hard, Jack,' laughed Caroline. 'I promise even you'll be able to manage it!'

'Even me, eh?' said Jack, with a broad smile.

Caroline pursed her lips. She *really* had to stop insulting the poor guy. It wasn't *his* fault that she was still busy overcompensating for her enormous crush by being an even more enormous cowbag!

'The lights have been on for a while now,' she said, ploughing on and doing her best to ignore the way his wide smile was making her stomach turn somersaults.

'So I'll turn them off, and then you turn them back on. Ceremonially.'

Jack let out a snort of laughter and Caroline frowned. 'What? It's tradition!'

'Okay – so I'd *ceremonially* turn them back on,' said Jack, his eyes twinkling. 'Then what?

'Then you'd need to say a few words,' said Caroline, bracing for his reaction. She had a feeling that this was where he was going to put his foot down and tell her to sling her hook. If Jack was here to lay low, there was no way he was going to agree to make a speech in front of the whole town, was there?!

'So… when's this little shindig meant to be happening?' said Jack.

Caroline blinked. He still hadn't said no… not outright anyway.

'It'll have to be soon,' she said.

'Yeah, I gathered that much!' laughed Jack. 'What with Christmas being just a week away!'

'I know,' said Caroline. 'Total nightmare. It's not usually this late – I had to cancel the first time around because of a storm, and I haven't dared to set another date until I can find a willing victim… erm… I mean… volunteer.'

'Well, that makes sense, I guess,' said Jack, taking a thoughtful sip of his coffee. 'You know, I've always thought the night before Christmas Eve is magical – and perfect for this sort of thing. Everyone's in full-on festive mode, but they haven't started to retreat into their little family groups yet.'

'I'd be up for doing it that night... if you fancy the job?' said Caroline, crossing her fingers under the table.

'Mmm...' said Jack, turning his coffee cup in little circles on the table. 'I'm not sure...'

'What's holding you back?' said Caroline. 'Because if I can fix it, I will!'

'Well... I guess I'm worried I might be a bit of a distraction to the main event.'

'Jack,' laughed Caroline, 'you kind of *would* be the main event!'

'And there lies the rub!' said Jack. 'It shouldn't be about me. I've been pretty careful not to let anyone know I'm here... so I don't want everyone to think I'm just doing it as some kind of publicity stunt. Plus, if I'm honest, I could really do without a bunch of press turning up and camping outside the house while I'm trying to enjoy a quiet Christmas. That'd suck.'

'Yeah, that *would* suck,' Caroline nodded. 'How about... if I promise not to publicise the fact that you're going to be there? I won't even mention it. You can just rock up on the night and give everyone the surprise of their lives!'

'You'd be up for that?' said Jack, looking surprised. 'I mean, whenever I've been asked to do this sort of thing before, it's always been about making as big a splash as possible. Maximum buzz. Maximum mudslinging in advance in the hope of receiving more inches in the celebrity rags.'

'Of course I'm up for it,' said Caroline. 'I could just bill you as "home-grown talent" or something like that.'

'Oh, so you *do* think I'm talented, then?' said Jack, with a cheeky grin.

'It's not about what *I* think,' said Caroline, rolling her eyes. 'I love Crumbleton – I want everyone to have a nice time and give them a Christmas surprise… and you'd *definitely* fit that bill.'

'That's really sweet,' said Jack.

'So, you'll do it?' said Caroline, looking hopeful.

'I'll think about it,' said Jack.

'How long for?' said Caroline. 'I hate to rush you here, but you were the one who pointed out Christmas is just a week away!'

'Well… I reckon I've got tonight at the very least,' said Jack. 'You're not going to be organising much this afternoon either way.'

'Why?' said Caroline.

Jack simply pointed over towards the window.

Caroline peered over and gasped. In the short time they'd been chatting, the snow seemed to have redoubled its efforts. There was a positive flurry of white flakes swirling just beyond the glass. She climbed to her feet and wandered over to take a look out across the garden.

'Even the beach is turning white!' she said.

She'd never seen anything like it. Not only had most

of the garden's features been softened under a ridiculous amount of snow, even the salty, golden sand beyond was busy turning into a blank white canvas.

'Am I caught in some kind of time warp?' said Caroline. 'I have only been here about half an hour, right?'

'Uh huh,' said Jack, looking amused.

'And this has happened in that time?'

'Yep,' said Jack.

'Shiiiiit,' breathed Caroline. 'How the hell am I meant to get back to Crumbleton?'

'Maybe it looks worse than it is?' said Jack. 'Let's have a look at your car.'

Abandoning their coffee cups on the slate island, they both trundled out of the kitchen towards the front door. Opening it, Caroline was met with a blast of icy air. Snowflakes found her face and settled on her nose and eyelashes.

'My car...?' she gasped.

'I'm sure it's out there,' chuckled Jack. 'Somewhere!'

The movie star at her side seemed to be missing the seriousness of the situation. Her little car was nothing more than a snowy white bump on the driveway.

'How on earth am I meant to get home?' she said. 'Have you got anything I can use to dig it out with?'

'Erm... I don't know,' said Jack. 'Even if I did, you know that's a terrible idea, right?'

'I'm stronger than I look,' said Caroline. 'I can totally clear a path down to the road.'

'And then what?' demanded Jack. 'Even if the main road is clear enough – which I doubt – there's no way the road across the marshes is going to be passable... not if the stuff's literally settling on the beach!'

'But—' said Caroline.

'No buts!' said Jack, suddenly sounding more than a little bit stubborn. 'It'll be feet deep by the time you get out of the driveway. You're just going to have to stay put with me until it clears up.'

'You...?' Caroline turned away from the white mound that was her car to stare at Jack.

Jack Jones, Hollywood's golden boy, had just invited her to stay safe with him at his house. Jack Jones, the guy she'd torn to shreds in the paper on multiple occasions.

No... not Jack Jones. Just Jack.

'You don't mind?' she said, re-finding her voice with an effort.

Jack shrugged. 'I wouldn't have asked you if I did,' he said. 'And... I'm not sure I have that much choice in the matter. Nor do you, come to that.'

'Well... okay, thanks,' said Caroline.

'Can we go back inside now?' said Jack with an exaggerated shiver. 'I think I'm starting to get frostbite.'

'That's your own idiotic fault for leaving a perfectly lovely, warm house to go swimming in the snow!' laughed Caroline, following Jack back inside and breathing a sigh of relief as he closed the front door.

'Don't knock it till you've tried it,' said Jack,

shooting her a wicked grin. 'I'm going again in a mo, and this time you're coming with me. I've got a guest wetsuit upstairs.'

'You're joking?!' gasped Caroline. 'Not on your nelly!'

For one thing, she had absolutely no desire to dive into the ice-cold waves while a snowstorm whipped around above her. For another… there was *no way* she was going to show Jack Jones what she looked like in a skin-tight wetsuit. Not on their first date.

Not that this was a date, of course!

'Okay… you need to breathe,' chuckled Jack. 'I'm joking, so you don't need to look like you're going to pass out from shock!'

'Don't exaggerate,' huffed Caroline.

'Wouldn't dream of it,' said Jack, shooting her a wink as he led the way back along the hall, this time heading for the living room. 'I only speak the truth.'

Staring at the beautiful, tiled floor as she went, Caroline did her best to pull herself together. Part of her *wished* she could just make a break for it and head back to her little flat in Crumbleton. She'd said her piece and now she just had to wait for an answer… and she didn't need to do that here. It looked like Jack had a bit of a knack for pressing her buttons, and she wasn't *entirely* sure she wanted them pressed!

Who was she kidding?! Jack could press any button of hers he liked!

Nearly giggling out loud at the thought, Caroline

quickly pulled in a deep breath and gave herself a little shake. She didn't know what she'd done to deserve it, but it looked like Christmas had come early. She was going to spend the afternoon with Jack Jones, for heaven's sake! Jack Jones... who'd told her to call him just... Jack!

Weird!

This was basically a dream come true – an all-access pass to her monster crush!

No. She shouldn't even think those words while she was in his house!

The poor guy probably had to put up with girls swooning all over him left, right and centre. She didn't want to become one of them. She'd keep control of herself and do her best to remain professional about the whole thing.

'Feel free to curl back up on your favourite sofa!' said Jack with a cheeky smile. 'I'll grab our drinks from the kitchen'.

Huh, so much for professional!

Caroline nodded and sank down into the cushions. Instead of leaning back and curling her feet up underneath her like she really wanted to, she remained bolt upright, her ankles crossed in a ladylike fashion.

Her nerves zinged as she glanced across at the windows, but there wasn't really much to see. It was practically a whiteout by this point as a winter wonderland developed beneath its cloudy blankets.

The wood burner crackled, pulling her attention

back into the room, and she fought a yawn that did its best to body snatch her. Caroline was caught somewhere between wanting to relax into the weird turn of fate that had literally stranded her in Jack's house, and not daring to in case she did or said something completely mortifying.

More mortifying than what she'd already done and said, that was!

'Here!' said Jack, shuffling back into the room bearing their two steaming mugs in front of him. 'I took the liberty of making us a fresh cup... the other ones had gone cold.'

'Oh!' said Caroline, surprised at his thoughtfulness. 'Well, thanks.' She took the jaunty painted mug from him and balanced it on her knee.

'So... here's a question,' said Jack. He was still standing in front of her, looking adorably awkward - about as far from a swaggering Hollywood actor as he could get. 'Are you any good at decorating Christmas trees?'

Caroline blinked, taken by surprise at the unexpected question.

'Erm... I wouldn't say good,' hedged Caroline, 'but I'm definitely enthusiastic!'

'Excellent,' said Jack, 'because I keep trying to finish off this whopper, but I keep getting distracted.'

'Who gets distracted decorating a Christmas tree?' laughed Caroline.

'Someone who's half in a different time zone, who's

still living out of suitcases, and whose house is in a bit of a wreck because he hasn't dealt with unpacking yet?' said Jack.

'Good answer,' said Caroline, scrambling to her feet and doing her best not to spill her coffee in the process. 'I guess I should warn you – I haven't had much practice. I've just got one of those little artificial tinsel trees at home. If you're expecting some kind of designer styling, I'm not your girl.'

'Hey – zero expectations here,' said Jack, shooting her an easy smile. 'I just want to use up all my tinsel.'

'Who said you're going to be in charge of the tinsel?' demanded Caroline.

'Oh, I see how it's going to be!' said Jack, laughing as he led the way over to the ginormous tree in the corner. 'Something tells me you like to be in charge?'

'Ah good,' said Caroline, grinning at him, 'you figured that out nice and fast!'

Jack rolled his eyes good-naturedly.

'May I?' she said, eyeballing a large cardboard box that looked like it was still stuffed to the gunnels with baubles, tinsel and fake holly.

'Be my guest,' said Jack. 'Which you are… obviously!'

'Awesome,' said Caroline, kneeling down next to the box and then staring up at the tree with its puny smattering of baubles dotted half-heatedly here and there. 'See… I'd say you've already made a rookie mistake.'

'Oh yeah?' said Jack.

'Uh-huh,' said Caroline, reaching into the box. 'Everyone knows you need to start with these!' She pulled out a long, tangled string of multicoloured lights and waved them at him. 'Come on, grab an end - we've got some untangling to do!'

CHAPTER 6

JACK

'Now that really is quite something,' said Jack, stepping back from the big bushy tree after hanging the final glittering icicle in place. It had been quite a job to find an empty branch for it.

'Not bad, eh?' said Caroline, staring at their handiwork.

Jack nodded slowly. He'd never had so much fun decorating a Christmas tree in his life… though, if he was being honest, he hadn't actually decorated an entire tree since he was a kid.

He'd certainly never had the pleasure while he'd been living in America. His handlers had brought in Festive Designers for such things, and the most he'd been allowed to do was dangle a ceremonial candy cane here and there at charity dos.

Working side by side with Caroline had been unexpectedly fun. They'd spent the last hour squabbling playfully over who was in charge of the tinsel and what order everything should go in. It felt like they'd known each other forever. There was an ease and a tension between them all at once. His fingers had brushed hers when they'd both reached into the box at the same time, and a tingle of electricity had leapt between them, making his stomach flip. It had been as much as he could do to draw breath.

'Well... I think we're done,' said Caroline.

'I think you're right,' said Jack. 'Just as well, really, considering there isn't room for anything else on there, even if we tried!'

'Good point,' said Caroline, reaching out and hooking a loop of tinsel a little higher. 'One more job left to do, though.'

'The lights,' said Jack. 'You want to do the honours?'

Caroline shook her head. 'I think you need all the practice you can get, don't you?' she said, shooting him a cheeky smile. 'Think of it as an audition for the starring role.'

'An audition?' said Jack, raising his eyebrows. 'I thought you were the one here *begging* me to do it.'

'You thought wrong,' said Caroline. 'This role is a privilege... one you have to earn.'

'There's the Caroline Cook I know and... am mildly terrified of!' laughed Jack.

Caroline rolled her eyes. 'You do realise you're doing the full-name thing with *me* now, right?'

'What can I say? It's catching!' said Jack. 'Okay, give me a sec to get into character here...'

'What character?' said Caroline. 'Big knobhead actor?'

'Ouch!' laughed Jack, just as Caroline clapped her hand over her mouth.

'I'm so sorry,' she muttered through her fingers. 'I don't know what's wrong with me. It's like I can't turn it off!'

Jack just grinned and shook his head. 'Ready – for the best big knobhead actor you've ever seen?'

'I'll be the judge of that!' said Caroline, smiling at him, clearly relieved that he didn't care about her less-than-cosy commentary.

'Okay, here goes,' said Jack. He let his smile drop before turning his head this way and that, making a show of stretching his neck.

'Lord, give me strength!' muttered Caroline, as Jack rolled his shoulders and stretched his arms across his chest as though preparing for a race.

Buoyed by her reaction, Jack started to ham it up for all he was worth, reaching for his toes and then bouncing a couple of times before dropping into a lunge.

'Are you quite finished?' giggled Caroline.

'Hmm, not sure,' said Jack, straightening up before adding in a side-bend. He promptly received Caroline's elbow in the ribs.

'Oof!' he laughed, rubbing the spot.

'Get on with it,' said Caroline. 'With that performance, I'll be roping you into the Crumbleton Panto if you don't watch out!'

'Oh no you won't!' said Jack gamely.

'Oh yes I... actually... let's not go there,' said Caroline. 'Turn those lights on already, man!'

Jack gave her a little salute before dropping to his knees and groping through the prickly branches until his fingers found the switch.

'Ooooh!' cried Caroline. 'They're absolutely gorgeous!'

Jack scrambled back to his feet, brushing a few stray needles from his jeans as he went. Then he stared up at the tree and nodded. The multi-coloured, twinkling lights set the whole thing off perfectly. Suddenly, the room felt like home, and for the first time this year, he really believed that Christmas was waiting for him just around the corner.

A sudden warm tightness in his chest took Jack by surprise, and he blinked rapidly, clearing his throat.

'I'd like to thank my agent,' he said, instinctively covering the weird swell of emotion with more impromptu ridiculousness. 'Of course, I couldn't have done this without my fans. But more than anything else, I'd like to thank Caroline Cook. Her reporting might be a bit on the wild side, but her heart is well and truly in the right place, and she knows how to hang a mean bauble...'

'Bloody actors!' huffed Caroline, rolling her eyes at him.

Jack grinned at her. 'Seriously though,' he said, letting his voice drop to its normal pitch, 'thank you for this. I think I'd still have had a half-naked tree when New Year rolled around if you hadn't turned up.'

'You're very welcome,' said Caroline. 'It was fun. But... now that's done, I think I'd better see if things have eased off out there. With any luck, I might be able to get home...'

Jack nodded, doing his best to ignore the sinking sensation in his stomach. He didn't actually *want* her to leave... which was a bit of an odd realisation, considering the circumstances.

The pair of them moved to the window, and Jack couldn't help but laugh.

'That'd be a no, then,' said Caroline.

'Erm... yeah,' said Jack. 'That snow's being far too enthusiastic for its own good... and I reckon if the beach is still white, the roads *definitely* will be too.' He raised his hand and ruffled his hair, a sense of unaccustomed nervousness washing over him. 'I guess you're stuck with me.'

'Nope,' said Caroline, shaking her head, 'I'm afraid it's you who's stuck with me. But I promise I'll try not to be too much of a pain in the bum.'

'I'll hold you to that!' said Jack. 'Anyway, it's just as well I've got plenty of food in. If this had happened yesterday, we'd be sharing half a dry crust of bread and a bowl of soggy cornflakes – without milk!'

Caroline crinkled her nose. 'Wow, how the other half live!'

'Right?' chuckled Jack. 'Not today, though. We'll feast like the three kings, thanks to Brian.'

'Brian?' said Caroline. 'You mean Brian Singer?'

'My saviour!' Jack nodded. 'I'm not sure what I'd have done without him since buying this place. He brings me shopping so that I don't have to out myself by visiting the supermarket or ordering online. Plus, he ferries me around whenever I'm in town. The man's a saint, and he never tells anyone I'm here… well… not until today, I guess.'

'Oh, it wasn't Brian who told me!' said Caroline quickly.

'Really?' said Jack, looking sceptical. 'Trish then?'

'No chance. Neither of them would dream of it! Lee, however…' she glanced at Jack's new bookcase.

'Ohhhh!' said Jack as the penny dropped. 'I didn't think he recognised me!'

'Erm… yeah, he did,' said Caroline. 'And Lee is an idiot. Much as I love him…'

'You do?' said Jack. This admission didn't make his stomach flip. Instead, it dropped right through the centre of the earth, and the Christmas lights suddenly lost all their charm.

'We've known each other forever,' said Caroline.

'Oh. Well... that's nice.' Jack cringed. His voice had just gone all hard and cold.

'It's the only reason I let the plonker get away with being... well... himself!' laughed Caroline.

'So... how long have you two been together?' said Jack, turning to head back through to the kitchen. Suddenly, he needed to get away from the festive scene.

'Wait – EEW!' said Caroline, grabbing at his hand and swinging him back towards her. 'Together?!'

'You and Lee,' said Jack. 'I mean, you said...'

'Hell no!' Caroline wrinkled her nose. 'That would be like... EWW! He's like my brother. No – not even that. Like an annoying cousin who turns up and ruins your Barbie dolls. I would never, *ever* kiss...'

Jack started to laugh as Caroline tailed off and started to make barfing motions at the floor.

'Okay, okay,' he chuckled. 'My bad! I got the wrong end of the stick.'

'Wrong end of the entire forest, more like!' said Caroline, staring at him with horror still in her eyes.

'And you think *I'm* the drama queen,' said Jack, shaking his head.

'At least give me some credit for taste,' huffed Caroline.

'So... your husband's cute then?' said Jack, trying to make his tone light and failing completely.

'Husband?' hooted Caroline. 'I'm not married. Or living with anyone. Or in a relationship... unless you count my ailing spider plant?'

'I don't think anyone would count that,' said Jack, a broad smile spreading over his face. For some strange reason, his heart had just pogoed back into position.

This didn't make any sense at all. Caroline was larger than life, stubborn, bossy… and… well… she was doing something to him. Jack hadn't felt this giddy in… hell, he'd never felt this giddy! Not when he'd won his first award. Not even when he'd stepped onto his first film set.

'So… what should we do now?' he said, his voice strangely husky.

'Got any more trees that need decorating?' said Caroline. 'I quite liked making myself useful!'

'Sadly not,' said Jack, ruffling his hair awkwardly. 'You know, it's a shame you're not an interior designer. I've got no idea where to put the shelves your *boyfriend* delivered.'

'Again – EEW!' said Caroline with an exaggerated shudder before she pottered towards the new bookshelf and ran her fingers over the glossy wood. 'So… is this your Christmas gift to yourself?'

'Not exactly,' said Jack, 'but it's much needed.'

'To hold all the Christmas cards from your swooning fans?' said Caroline.

'No, smartass,' said Jack. 'To hold all my scripts. They're getting everywhere… and I need to get them in some kind of order. I've already managed to cover them in coffee rings and goodness knows what else.'

'Well, I'm definitely not an interior designer,' said Caroline, 'but I'm happy to help!'

'You're my guest,' said Jack. 'I'm not putting you to work!'

'For one thing, you've already done that with your Christmas tree,' she laughed. 'And for another – I don't mind. Besides, it'll be easier to move it around with two of us.'

Jack nodded. He couldn't exactly fault that logic.

'So... any idea where you want it?' she prodded.

'Not too near the wood burner for obvious reasons,' said Jack.

'And I'd suggest not too near the windows either,' said Caroline. 'All those scripts will just remind you of work instead of letting you enjoy the view.'

'Good point!' said Jack. He hadn't even thought of that. Work already took up more than its fair share of his life.

'It would fit best just over there near the door,' said Caroline.

'What, right in front of the light switch?' laughed Jack.

'Oh... yeah,' said Caroline. 'Maybe not. Erm... how about we shift that sofa into the room by about two feet? You'll barely notice it's moved, but then you can pop the shelves against the wall over there.'

Jack stared at the spot and then back at Caroline. 'You might just be a genius.'

'Might?' huffed Caroline. 'It was proven years ago - you just need to catch up.'

She winked at him, and Jack felt something inside him melt.

'Alright,' he said. 'Let's give it a go.'

With more than a little grunting, the pair of them managed to slide the sofa away from the wall. Then they shuffled the heavy shelves into place before standing back to admire their handiwork.

'What do you think?' said Caroline, glancing from him to the shelves and then back again.

'It's perfect,' said Jack with a little shrug. 'Now we just need to fill it up!'

CHAPTER 7

CAROLINE

They started in the kitchen - the pair of them scooping up armfuls of the printed and bound scripts that seemed to be balanced on every available surface.

Jack muttered an apology with every trip they made from the kitchen to the living room, but Caroline was thoroughly enjoying having something practical to do.

'Just bung 'em on the floor for now,' said Jack. 'I need to sort through them and get them into some kind of order.'

'Okay,' said Caroline. 'Hey... do you want to do that while I grab the rest for you? You said there are more upstairs?'

'You don't have to do that,' said Jack with a sheepish expression. 'You've done enough already.'

'Don't be daft,' said Caroline. 'I'm having fun!'

'But they're in my bedroom,' said Jack.

'Doesn't worry me,' she said with a shrug. 'As long as *you* don't mind. I mean… how often will I get the chance to snoop around a film star's house?'

'Hmm… snoop around? See, you're not selling me on this plan,' said Jack. 'Are you wearing a hidden video camera? Oh God, you're livestreaming this whole thing, aren't you?!'

Caroline glared at him in indignation… and then started to laugh. He was pulling her leg. Of course he was.

'As much as I'm sure a livestream from inside Jack Jones's house would go down a storm, there's no way I'd do that to you – or anybody else for that matter.'

'Good to know,' he laughed.

'I'm just nosy,' she added with a shrug. 'But don't worry, I get it if you don't want to set me loose!'

'Have at it,' said Jack easily. 'I don't mind. But I apologise in advance for the mess.'

'You don't have any skeletons up there, do you?' said Caroline.

'Have a look for yourself… though if you *do* find any, I'd appreciate a heads up,' said Jack. 'I'm more of a rom-com guy than a horror fan.'

'You know, it would be *brilliant* if you made another romcom!' said Caroline.

'Not wooden and three-star?'

'Stop digging for compliments,' she snorted, clambering to her feet and heading for the door before he could change his mind about the whole thing.

'Feel free to have a good look around while you're up there,' said Jack. 'My bedroom's the second door on the left across the hall. If you get lost, gimme a shout and I'll come to your rescue.'

'My hero!'

Caroline practically skipped out of the room and then made her way straight for the broad, sweeping staircase. She couldn't quite believe that he'd agreed to her mooching around his house unsupervised... and she was going to make the most of it before he came to his senses.

'I can't believe I'm going to get to look inside Jack Jones's bedroom!' she breathed, jogging up the staircase and admiring the beautiful light fitting at the top that dripped pendant bulbs in gleaming waves.

Before heading across to Jack's bedroom, Caroline peeped inside a couple of rooms whose doors stood ajar. The first was set up as a little reading nook. The walls were lined with well-worn paperbacks, and there was a large, squashy-looking armchair and footstool arranged in front of the window. The second was clearly a guest bedroom – complete with a huge four-poster bed.

'Wow!' she whispered. If this was the spare bedroom, she could only imagine what the master one must be like...

Scuttling further along the hall, Caroline pushed her way inside Jack's bedroom. It was just as large and airy as the room she'd just seen, but a whole lot messier!

'Tut tut, Mr Film Star,' she muttered, stooping to pick up a damp, slightly sandy beach towel from the carpet at the foot of the bed. Giving it a little shake, she draped it over the corner of the half-open wardrobe door so that it could dry off.

'Right… scripts…' she muttered, letting her eyes scan the room.

It was beautiful, despite the chaos of half-unpacked cases, discarded clothing and abandoned scripts lying higgledy-piggledy all over the place. Just like the spare room, it was light and airy, with high ceilings and long, luxurious curtains that framed the view straight out over the beach.

Right in the centre of the room, the vast bed boasted red and green tartan blankets. Jack clearly had a thing for Christmassy comfort. She'd bet anything that he had a pair of special crimbo PJs tucked away somewhere too. She'd have to ask him.

'Or maybe not,' whispered Caroline.

She quickly fanned her face with her hands as blood rushed to her cheeks at the thought of Jack in his PJs. She knew it was the biggest cliché ever… but it was impossible *not* to have a crush on the man.

Now she'd actually met Jack… well, he was even more attractive in person. It didn't have anything to do with his celebrity status, either. The man was clearly as big a dork as she was - that cringey speech, and the way he'd fought her for his favourite Christmas ornament. Caroline knew her little crush was rapidly blooming into something monumental.

'Don't be an idiot!' she muttered.

After all, dork or not, Jack *was* an international film star. There was no way he'd be interested in a small-town newspaper reporter with nothing to offer other than a half-dead spider plant.

'Come on, woman, focus!' she muttered. There wasn't any point worrying about something that was so far from being possible, it was almost funny. She needed to grab the scripts and take them back down to Jack before he sent out a search party.

Jack hadn't been lying, the scripts really were everywhere. She picked up four from his bedside table, then gathered another bunch that were lying scattered across his bed and the floor next to it.

When she was pretty sure she'd managed to find them all, she eyeballed the door on the far side of the room.

Cupboard?

Pottering over, she opened it and gasped.

Nope... not a cupboard!

It was the most gorgeous ensuite she'd ever had the pleasure of clapping eyes on. Not only was there a shower big enough to fit about twenty people – with multiple heads and an entire shelf groaning with products - there was also a roll-topped bath right in the middle of the space. And... it was made of copper.

'And there I was thinking you were actually quite normal!' murmured Caroline, moving over to the little wooden table that stood next to the bath and grabbing yet another script that lay – half open – between a shaving brush and the bottles of soap and shampoo.

Half wishing she could dive right into that tub herself, Caroline gave it one last, longing look before deciding it was time to head back downstairs with her finds.

❄

'How's it going?' said Jack, looking up at her from his cross-legged position on the floor.

He was surrounded by several piles of scripts, and it looked like he was only about halfway through sorting through the ones they'd brought through from the kitchen.

'These are all from your bedroom,' said Caroline, adding her armful to the mound he was still working his way through. 'How's it going with you?'

'Remakes, sequels, prequels,' said Jack, tapping his way clockwise around the piles. 'Fourth in the series and the first one was awful. Then this one's already onto its seventh director, and this one means six months living in a tent in the Arctic.'

Caroline scrunched up her nose and shivered. 'Plenty of snow here, you don't need to go to the Arctic!'

'My thoughts entirely!' said Jack. 'Though I'm not sure which pile to add it to.'

'How about a whole new section based on geographical location?' she said.

'I like it!' laughed Jack. 'We'll have a shelf for *too cold to consider*.'

Caroline snorted. 'So... how many of these are you actually interested in?'

'Erm, to be fair I haven't done much more than glance at them when they arrive, but based on first impressions... that's this pile here,' said Jack, patting an empty patch of carpet.

'Not sure that counts as a pile,' said Caroline, sinking down next to him.

'Yeah.' Jack let out a weary sigh and ran his fingers through his hair. 'I'm not really sure what the future holds for me right now if I'm honest. I might just hang out here for a bit and see what happens.'

'Sounds good to me,' said Caroline.

'Why are you smiling?' said Jack, narrowing his eyes at her.

'I was just thinking I'd like the chance to get to know you better.'

The words were out of her mouth before she could stop them. Caroline blinked in surprise and mild confusion.

So much for playing it cool!

'I'd like that too,' said Jack, shifting slightly and looking adorably shy for a split second. 'I've always come here when I've wanted to go into hiding, but this time things feel different for some reason. It'd be nice to meet some people at last. I just… don't want it to become a big deal, you know?'

Caroline nodded.

'Plus, I don't really know where to start,' he added.

'Well, if you want people to get to know you, you're talking to the right person,' said Caroline.

'I didn't mean doing an interview in the paper!' laughed Jack.

'Neither did I!' said Caroline, clutching her heart in mock outrage. 'As if!'

'Uh huh?!' said Jack.

'Well… not this time, anyway. I just mean… basically I know everyone in Crumbleton. I can fill you in on who's who and maybe introduce you around a bit if you want to come out of hiding.'

The temptation to cross her fingers was overwhelming, but she managed to sit still, watching Jack's face intently.

'Well… I have to admit, I might already know a bit more about local goings-on than you think,' said Jack.

'Brian Singer keeping you in the loop?' she said.

'In a way,' said Jack with a small smile. 'He sends me a copy of the Crumbleton Times every week!'

'He does?' gasped Caroline.

'I've got to keep an eye on what mean things you've been saying about me somehow,' he laughed. 'You know… just in case I need to get my lawyers involved.'

Caroline dropped her face into her hands. She was going for dramatic effect, but it also helped her hide the blush of pure mortification that had just stained her cheeks. She really *had* been quite mean, hadn't she?!

'Don't worry,' said Jack, giving her arm a gentle nudge with his. 'It was good for my ego – and fun to see what you came up with next.'

Caroline peeped at him through her fingers and was relieved to see a broad grin still firmly on his face. She quickly sent up a prayer of thanks that she'd somehow managed to choose to insult one of the few megastars who didn't seem to take himself too seriously.

'Okay – fill me in on a few things,' said Jack. 'Is the guy who got walloped by that bride's bouquet doing okay?'

'How'd you know about that?' said Caroline. 'I didn't cover that story in the end!'

'Brian mentioned it in an email,' said Jack.

'Murray's fine,' said Caroline. 'Happily in love with the florist responsible, in fact!'

'You're joking?' said Jack.

'Dead serious,' said Caroline. 'Milly moved into his boat on the marshes, and the pair of them are sickeningly loved up.'

'Aww,' said Jack. 'And how's the museum fund doing.'

'Wow, you really have done your homework!' said Caroline. 'Again, really well. The tennis tournament made a ton of cash, and then there was a whopping anonymous donation that really helped.'

'I know,' said Jack.

'Don't tell me Brian filled you in on that too,' said Caroline, cocking her head curiously.

'He didn't,' said Jack. 'You... erm... mentioned it in the paper.'

Caroline peered intently at his face. 'Waaaait!' she gasped.

'Anyway,' said Jack, clearing his throat, 'was this all the scripts?'

'Don't go changing the subject on me, Jones!' she said, her eyes wide. 'That was you, wasn't it?'

'I have no idea what you mean,' said Jack lightly, flipping through a script as if his life depended on it.

'It was! I knew it!!' squealed Caroline. 'Admit it!'

'No comment,' said Jack, shooting her a small smile.

'Why on earth didn't you put your name against it?' said Caroline. 'If you want to get on the right side of the locals, something like that would *definitely* add to your street cred.'

'I'm not saying I *did* donate that money,' said Jack, 'but *if* I did - it's not about me. It was something important to Crumbleton... and definitely *not* some kind of publicity stunt!'

'But—'

'And that's only if it *was* me,' he added. 'Which I'm not saying it was.'

'Fine. Fair enough,' said Caroline. 'But... if it *was*

you, I know everyone in Crumbleton would want me to say thank you.'

'I'm sure whoever it was would be grateful. Now which pile should I add this one to?' he said, holding up the script, clearly keen to change the subject.

'What's it about?' said Caroline.

'Zombie dogs taking over the world,' said Jack.

'That would be... let me think... oh right – the bin pile!'

CHAPTER 8

JACK

Jack couldn't believe how fast the time was disappearing. With the heavy blanket of clouds still covering the horizon, the daylight had faded fast.

'I'm so glad you didn't try to drive home!' said Jack, tugging the heavy living room curtains closed to keep the room nice and toasty.

'Erm… yeah,' said Caroline, nodding from her perch on the old sofa. 'I think I'd be stranded somewhere out on the marshes right about now… and I really don't fancy that much. For one thing, I don't even have a blanket in the car, and for another… no food!'

Jack grinned at her as the statement elicited a rumble from the vicinity of her stomach.

'Oh my god,' she laughed, clutching her belly. 'Don't tell me you heard that?!'

He nodded. 'Sorry.'

'Smooth!'

Jack laughed. 'Well, thanks to Brian, I can do something about that.'

'I can't believe I have to slum it here with you instead of going back to my flat,' said Caroline with a sigh. 'I mean - beachside house… film star – what a let-down!'

'I'm just Jack,' he said. 'I might be a sub-par actor, but I promise to feed you. Is there anything else I can get you, though? Anything you need? It looks like you're going to be staying the night.'

Caroline paused and Jack raised his eyebrows at the look of longing on her face. He swallowed.

'Erm… what? What is it?' he said, his stupid voice coming out all husky again.

'Well… I happened to spot your frankly monstrous bathtub while I was gathering up the scripts earlier,' she said.

Jack nodded as his brain scrambled to catch up with what she was saying. His mind had been wandering off in unexpected directions. He blinked hard, focussing on her lips and forcing himself to listen to what she was actually saying.

'Would it be incredibly cheeky… I mean, as I'm stuck here anyway?'

He'd definitely missed a bit of that sentence. 'Erm… you fancy a dip?' he hazarded a guess.

'Only if you don't mind?' she said quickly. 'My place has just got this incredibly pathetic shower. It's like standing under a dripping tap! You can barely turn around in it, and if you drop the soap, you've got to open the door to give yourself enough room to pick it up again and then the whole room fills with steam and—'

'It's fine!' he said, his voice coming out in a kind of high-pitched squeak as he did his best not to picture Caroline reaching for a bar of soap in a steamy bathroom. 'Sure… have a dip… of course!'

'You certain?' said Caroline, raising one eyebrow at him. 'Sure it's not… weird?'

Jack did his best to arrange his face into something natural while he dragged his thoughts firmly back out of the gutter. 'Of course not. Go for it.'

If nothing else, it would give him the chance to get his head back on straight.

'Thank you!' she said, hopping to her feet and following him out into the hallway.

'Oh – erm… towels,' he said, doing his best not to think too hard about the fact that Caroline would be lounging in his bath before too long. 'There's a cupboard just to the left when you go into the bathroom – there's a stack in there.'

'Non-sandy ones?' she said.

'With any luck!' said Jack. 'Enjoy. I'll rustle us up something to eat while you're in there.'

'Yay, even better,' said Caroline. 'You know… this is a pretty good hotel!'

Jack grinned at her and watched as she climbed up

to the first floor. He couldn't help himself – it was like he was rooted to the spot.

The minute Caroline disappeared around the corner, Jack gave himself a little shake and made a dash for the kitchen. He was sure he had plenty of time, but he wanted to pull together something a bit more impressive than his usual sandwich in front of the wood burner!

'Thank heavens for Brian!' he murmured, heading over to the fridge and opening the door.

It was packed to the gunnels with enough goodies to feed a family of five for the whole of Christmas. Brian had done a big enough shop that he could go to ground until the New Year if he wanted to…

'Right, let's see…' he said, rooting around on the shelves.

There must be *something* he could cook using this lot that would impress Caroline. *Not* that he was trying to impress her, of course. This wasn't a date, after all.

Or was it?!

Nope – definitely not a date.

'Stop being an idiot, man!' he huffed.

Jack had pretty much forgotten what it was like to go on a date… which was a bit weird considering the number of times over the last few years he'd had to pretend to be in love with various people in front of the camera. He hadn't even liked some of them!

He'd always been careful to keep the line drawn between work and real life. As much as it was his job to make things look as real as possible on set, he'd never played the flirting game with his co-stars... not like some of them did for the publicity. They played up to the media for all they were worth, and Jack knew for a fact that several of them tipped the paps off themselves when they wanted some decent headlines in the celebrity rags.

Jack had never craved the attention that went with the job. That was why he'd bought this house in Crumbleton Sands. It was his safe haven. Whenever he wanted peace and quiet and a dose of reality, it was good to know he could come here and decompress from the madness. Here, he could swim in the sea looking like a tadpole wearing a Santa hat, and it wouldn't be splashed all over the internet within seconds.

But... maybe he'd taken the whole isolation thing a little bit too far. It was one thing keeping his job and his private life separate, but it was another thing to completely cut himself off from the world to the point that loneliness had started to creep in like a bitter ache.

Caroline had turned up on his doorstep unannounced... and he'd let her in because – well – he'd simply been craving some human company.

Shock horror!

On top of that... she was even prettier in real life than she was in the photographs he'd seen online. He'd been intrigued to find out more about the funny, witty woman whose writing he'd been enjoying so much.

And now she's in your bath!

Realising he was still standing with the fridge door wide open, Jack let out a long sigh. He didn't have a clue what Caroline did or didn't like. There wasn't any point starting on food until he found out what she fancied.

'Only one way to do that!' he muttered.

Heading out of the kitchen, Jack jogged up the stairs and made his way towards his bedroom. The door was wide open – which was a blessing – at least it was one less thing to overthink!

Jack strode across the room, wincing at the sight of the sandy towel Caroline must have picked up and hung on the door of his wardrobe. Even worse, he realised there was still a discarded wetsuit in the corner of the ensuite. Ah well, it was too late to do anything about that right now.

Pausing right outside the door, he strained his ears. He could hear running water still sploshing into the tub.

'Caroline?' he called loudly.

There was a squeak, a splash, and then a flurry of movement.

'Yeah?!' came a surprised, decidedly flustered voice.

'Sorry!' he said. 'I didn't mean to make you jump. Don't worry... I'm not coming in. I was just wondering if there's anything you don't eat or... any... you know... dietary requirements?'

Jack winced. Caroline might be the surprised one,

but he was managing to get himself completely tongue-tied here.

'Nope,' she called, sounding decidedly relieved.

'At all?' said Jack, barely believing his ears.

'Nope – I'm easy,' said Caroline. 'I mean… I… erm… all food's good with me, thanks!'

Jack grinned. *What a pair!*

'Okay cool. Erm… have a good bath.'

He backed away from the door as fast as his feet could carry him – mainly because the temptation to ask if he could join her was almost overwhelming. Not that he'd *ever* summon the courage to do anything of the sort, of course!

Taking the steps two at a time, Jack blew out a sigh of relief as he put a bit of distance between himself and the overwhelming desire to do something *seriously* embarrassing.

At least he had his answer… it sounded like Caroline would basically eat anything he put in front of her! It was almost too easy. Jack didn't think he'd met anyone in years who didn't have some kind of food quirk. A lot of his co-stars had nutritionists who kept them on tight and extremely weird eating plans. He had to admit, it drained a lot of the fun out of eating out when the person across from you wouldn't order anything other than clear bone broth or a green smoothie!

Sliding to a halt in front of the fridge again, Jack promptly decided his best bet was to simply empty the contents onto the kitchen island so that they could just help themselves to anything they fancied. There was plenty of cheese, olives, cold meat, and chutney... in fact, Brian had clearly brought him the entire contents of Bendall's deli counter.

After opening everything up and arranging it all on the stoneware plates his agent had sent him as a housewarming gift, Jack turned to open the large brown paper bag with the Crumbleton Bakery logo on the front. He stuck his nose inside and sniffed hungrily.

Jack's stomach promptly growled as the scent of freshly baked bread almost made him pass out with joy. Was there a better smell than that – other than freshly ground coffee? He drew the large, round loaf out of the bag with a certain amount of reverence and set it on his wooden breadboard. Then he reached for the large, serrated knife and expertly sliced several generous chunks.

'Olive oil and balsamic!' he said, clicking his fingers and reaching for a dish so that he could slosh in the tasty mixture.

There, that would be perfect for some dipping action.

Along with the bread, Brian had collected a selection of cakes from the bakery. Flipping open the lid of the box, Jack stared at them hungrily. Doughnuts, stunningly iced cupcakes, gooey chunks of perfectly crusted lemon drizzle, and several stacks of cinnamon biscuits.

'Heaven,' he sighed. Then he promptly closed the

box again before temptation got the better of him. He'd keep them for a bit later – with any luck, a nice pudding surprise would earn him some literal brownie points from his guest.

Pausing for a moment to survey the impressive spread, Jack wracked his brain for anything missing. Salt, pepper, sauces, napkins, forks, knives, plates…

'Drinks, duh!' he muttered.

Damnit!

He should have asked Caroline what she fancied while he was up there. He *could* go back up… but no doubt she'd be in the tub by now, and the last thing he wanted to do was to make her feel uncomfortable. Besides, it was best if there was at least one floor between them while she was… disrobed!

He could just ask her what she fancied when she came down. He had white wine in the fridge… and there were beers… and some kind of cordial stuff…

'Okay, you're spiralling, man,' chuckled Jack. 'Stop being a knob!'

Grabbing a cube of cheese, he popped it into his mouth and chewed, just to give himself something to do.

Okay… maybe he'd put the kettle on… and open a bottle of red so that it could breathe. Then he'd have all bases covered.

CHAPTER 9

CAROLINE

*H*oly Santa Clause and all his reindeer, this was the most amazing bath she'd *ever* been in. It didn't even come close.

Of all the places to get stranded in a snowstorm, Caroline had to admit that Jack's house might just be right at the top of the list. Up to her neck in bubbles, there was a good chance she might have just died and gone to heaven.

Of course, it had taken her stupid pulse a while to calm down after Jack's impromptu visit... mainly because she'd had a hard time stopping herself from "accidentally" opening the ensuite door... just to see what happened.

Grinning at the thought, Caroline wriggled her toes in the warm, scented water. This. Was. Bliss. She hadn't realised just how much she'd missed having a bath -

and that was just a *normal* bath. This tub was on a whole other level!

Right now, she was staring out of a floor-to-ceiling window that looked out over a snow-covered beach. There wasn't much to see right now as it was almost dark, but she could hear the white-tipped waves as they crashed onto the sand.

Caroline leaned her head back and let her eyes drift closed as she did her best to let it all sink in. She was in a real movie star's house. Hell – not just his house, either – his private ensuite!

Jack was nothing like she'd dreaded him being. Far from an aloof, spoiled, entitled celeb, he was warm, funny… and seriously cute.

'And look what you wrote about him,' sighed Caroline, considering sinking under the bubbles with shame. She'd torn him apart. More than once. Despite the fact they'd already talked about it, and he'd joked and shrugged it off… Caroline couldn't help but feel sorry for it now.

She'd been wrong… especially about him buying this house. He was clearly desperate to make a proper home for himself here. It was also pretty obvious that he was having a hard time figuring out how to bridge the gap between being the Hollywood star who was hounded wherever he went, and the charming, funny, dorky man who cared enough to let her use his ensuite and check what she wanted for tea.

He'd asked her to help him decorate his Christmas

tree for heaven's sake. Could he be any sweeter? This was all her Christmas fantasies rolled into one.

As for the Crumbleton Christmas lights… she hadn't given them a second thought since she'd asked him if he'd be willing to help her out. She'd simply been having too much fun. It might have been a bit of an accident waiting to happen when she'd decided to drive to Crumbleton Sands with the snowstorm looming large, but it just went to show that not all accidents had to have sad endings.

'Don't think about endings!' she whispered through the steam.

❄

'Caroline?'

Caroline yawned, her eyes fluttering open.

'Helloo? You okay in there?'

A soft knock made Caroline sit bolt upright. Deep water swirled around her – and it was decidedly cooler than it had been a few seconds ago.

Or… maybe not just seconds?

'Hi!' she said quickly. 'Hi… won't be a sec!'

'There's no rush,' came Jack's amused voice from the other side of the door. 'I just wanted to check you hadn't managed to fall asleep and drowned yourself.'

'Nope – not drowned!' said Caroline. 'Still wide awake!'

'Well, that's good,' chuckled Jack. 'Because there's no

way the press would believe you'd died in some tragic, fluke accident.'

'Huh?!' said Caroline, sloshing to her feet and praying that he didn't burst in just to check she really was okay.

'Come on – do you really think anyone would believe there hadn't been some kind of foul play on my side of things after all those mean reviews you wrote about me?!' said Jack.

Caroline paused mid-way through wrapping the voluminous bath towel around herself and cocked her head. 'Okay… you might have a point there,' she said with a wry smile. 'Sorry to disappoint – but I'm alive and kicking. I'll be out in just a sec.'

'No worries,' said Jack. 'The food's ready when you are.'

'Okay – thanks!' said Caroline, pulling a face as she spotted how pruned her fingers were.

How long had she been in there?!

'Oh!' said Jack. 'What do you want to drink?'

'Erm…'

As much as she'd love nothing more than to settle down with a fancy-pants G&T right now, Caroline didn't want to give him the wrong impression. Besides, her stomach had started to growl with what could only be described as *vigour*. Maybe alcohol wasn't the best choice.

'Erm… what have you got?' she hedged.

'Wine… red, white. Beer, cider… whatever you

fancy really!' said Jack. 'I can re-boil the kettle if you'd prefer something hot?'

Re-boil?! How long had she been asleep?

'What are you going to have?' said Caroline, eyeballing her clothes. She could really do with getting dressed... but she didn't dare unwrap herself from the safety of the towel until he'd cleared off.

'Red wine I think,' said Jack.

'Count me in!' said Caroline. There. That was nice and easy. 'I'll be down in two secs.'

'Cool.'

Caroline strained her ears and listened as Jack's padding footsteps disappeared across the plush bedroom carpet on the other side of the door. Two seconds later, she caught the unmistakable clatter as he trotted back down the stairs.

'Seriously?' she muttered, yanking on her jeans while her hair dripped where the ends had rested in the bubbles. 'You fell asleep in his bathtub?! Smooth!'

As much as her growling stomach was urging her to hurry, Caroline took a few moments to make sure that the bath was clean and then took a peep in the mirror to check that her mascara hadn't slid halfway down her face. After swiping beneath her eyes for several seconds, she decided she'd have to do – after all, it wasn't as though she'd brought her makeup bag with her... more's the pity.

It didn't matter, anyway. She didn't need to worry about what Jack thought, did she?

Nope. Definitely not.

She didn't care what the cute, lovely film star thought of her one little bit.

'Liar,' she muttered, unlocking the door and padding across his bedroom. As she made her way past the bed, she spotted a script she must have missed earlier poking out from beneath the edge of the blankets.

Grabbing it and tucking it under her arm, Caroline hurried back downstairs, her stomach grumbling in anticipation as she went. It was only just dawning on her that she hadn't actually eaten anything since breakfast.

Rounding the corner into the kitchen, Caroline ground to a halt. The sight that greeted her made her hungry in a whole other way.

Jack was sitting at the kitchen island, perched on a stool, engrossed in a script he had open in front of him. It was chunky and closely typed, and he was wearing a pair of dark-framed reading glasses.

Holy moly!

How was it possible for the man to look even cuter *with* the glasses on?! They made him look… well… like *her* type of bloke. Whatever that was. He was completely adorable, and *hot!*

Caroline's knees promptly turned into jelly.

No way! Get a grip woman!

She wasn't about to fall for a film star who was only ever in the country for a few days a year. There was no way that'd work out – even if she wanted it to.

Which... she kind of did.

Caroline could feel a blush sneaking across her cheeks again. Suddenly, she wished she was back up in the ensuite so that she could hop into the shower and get a blast of cold water.

Who was she kidding, anyway? Jack Jones could have anyone he wanted. Why would he want to be with a small-town reporter with boundary issues, whose main source of intimate conversation was an ailing spider plant?

He wouldn't.

There wasn't any point thinking that way... even if it *was* a rather delicious fantasy! She'd just have to blame it on the Christmas lights and the fact that Jack had some old crooner on the record player making everything feel even more cosy and twinkly than it had before her bath!

'Oh hey!' said Jack, turning to find her staring at him. 'I didn't hear you come down... nice bath?'

'Maybe a bit too nice.' Caroline smiled at him, feeling suddenly shy. 'Sorry for keeping you waiting for so long.'

'Not at all,' said Jack. 'Anyway, I have to admit to snaffling a few bits of cheese and a couple of olives while you were up there!'

'I don't blame you!' said Caroline, her eyes roving over the vast spread he'd prepared for the first time.

'I know it's probably overkill for just the two of us,' said Jack, 'but I didn't know what you'd like, so I put out a bit of everything.'

'It looks amazing!' said Caroline, heading for one of the high stools. She avoided the one right next to him – there was far too much danger of "accidentally" brushing up against him if she sat there. Instead, she opted for the one around the corner. It afforded her a wonderful view of his face… and easy access to the cheese board too – bonus!

'Well… happy Christmas,' said Jack, passing her a plate.

'Thanks!' said Caroline. 'Though you're a bit early.'

'Only by a week,' said Jack with a shrug. 'Plus, I've got crackers, so that makes it official!'

Caroline wriggled with excitement as he passed one over.

'Are these fancy-pants ones with Fabergé eggs inside them?' she said.

'Erm… only if that's what they sell in Bendall's?' said Jack.

'Then probably not!' laughed Caroline. 'Here – pull!'

CHAPTER 10

JACK

It wasn't very often that Jack found himself speechless… but the sight of Caroline Cook standing in his kitchen doorway, all fresh and pink from her bath, with her hair slightly wavy from the steam – well it had nearly been enough to topple him right off his kitchen stool.

Now here she was, bouncing around with excitement after pulling a couple of the cheap Christmas crackers Brian had bought him as a surprise from Bendall's.

'Come out come out come out!' she chanted, rattling her end of the cracker in an attempt to encourage the cheap plastic toy out of its crepe paper prison.

Jack was busy pulling on an orange, tissue paper crown from his own cracker. He had no idea where his toy had gone… maybe it had flown across the kitchen and disappeared.

'Got ya!' cheered Caroline, as something small and pink whizzed from her cracker and skittered across the table between the cheese board and the jars of chutney.

'Ooh, classy!' chuckled Jack, fishing it out from its resting place underneath the bowl of olives. 'Here.'

He tipped it into Caroline's waiting palm, doing his best not to notice the zing of electricity that passed between their fingers at the contact.

'A pencil sharpener?' said Caroline.

'A pink, glittery, festive pencil sharpener I think you'll find!' said Jack.

'What did you get?' said Caroline, craning her neck.

'Nothing,' said Jack.

'Bet it's still stuck,' said Caroline. 'Give it here!'

Doing as he was told, Jack passed her the end of his cracker and watched in amusement as she gave it a good shake, sending something rattling onto his plate.

'There. Told you!' she crowed in triumph.

Sure enough, there was a large, rather ugly yellow plastic ring sitting right in the middle of his plate… complete with a sparkly plastic diamond.

'Wow, now that's expensive!' said Jack with a grin as he picked it up with exaggerated reverence. 'It's way too small to fit me – hold out your hand!'

Caroline raised an eyebrow and then extended her left hand, wiggling her fingers at him.

'Perfect fit,' he said, nestling it straight onto her wedding ring finger.

'Oh. Blimey!' said Caroline with a laugh of pure surprise.

Jack stared at her for a long moment. He had two choices… he could get all idiotic and tongue-tied, or let his inner actor take over.

'I've been planning to make an honest woman of you for the longest time,' he said, his voice low and booming as he smacked himself hard on the chest.

Caroline rolled her eyes, but he wasn't about to stop now.

'The time is finally right. I hope you'll take me, flaws and all. I know you deserve better, Imelda Gertrude Caroline the Great – but I hope you'll have me! We can make it work… I know we can. It'll take work… and at least eight or nine children!'

'Eight or nine?!' snorted Caroline, her shoulders shaking with giggles.

'You're spoiling the scene!' hissed Jack from behind his hand.

'*Fine!*' She sighed and cleared her throat. 'Jack Plonkerus Jones the third…'

They both winced as her accent fell somewhere between Texas and the Welsh Valleys.

'I do declare… I don't know what my daddy will say… nor my ten ex-husbands… but… but… I…' Caroline's words dissolved as her giggles took over.

Jack swiped at his eyes and took a swig of his wine.

Well, she might not have given him an answer to his imaginary proposal, but it didn't look like he was about to get that ring back in a hurry!

'I think we'd better eat something,' said Jack once they'd both had the chance to calm down a bit. 'Maybe it'll help that awful accent of yours!'

'Cheeky blighter,' said Caroline, with a loud huff. 'But yes please – pass me the Pringles?'

'First things first,' said Jack, handing her a paper napkin.

'Snowmen napkins, Jack?' she laughed. 'Really?'

'I'm sorry I didn't have my best linens ready,' he said with a broad grin. 'I didn't expect to have a special guest.'

'I guess I'll let you off then,' said Caroline, shooting him a wink. 'Besides, I quite like your festive side.'

'As long as it doesn't get out,' said Jack. 'I do have a reputation to uphold, you know!'

'Don't worry,' said Caroline, her voice suddenly serious. 'It won't.'

Jack shot her a look and then smiled. He didn't know why – but he trusted her completely. Maybe it was something to do with the fact that she'd already publicly torn him to shreds on multiple occasions. He had no doubt that she'd happily tell him to his face if she was angling for a story while she was there.

'Alrighty then,' said Jack, giving himself a little shake as he did his best to tear his eyes away from two little drops of water as they made their way slowly down the curve of her neck. 'If you think I'm going to let my guest dine on Pringles alone, then you have another thing coming!'

'Where do you want me to start then?' said Caroline.

'Anywhere!' said Jack.

'I'll have the pink Pringles then, please,' said Caroline with a grin.

Jack grudgingly handed them over and then grabbed her plate and started to pile it with a bit of everything within reach. Caroline guided him with little nods and shakes of the head as he went. He soon noticed that the shakes weren't exactly frequent, and were mainly aimed at anything containing chillies.

'There,' he said, popping the mounded plate down in front of her. 'For when you've finished your starter,' he chuckled, eyeballing the tube in her hand as she rummaged in its depths.

'Want one?' she said, crunching away happily.

Jack shook his head.

'Sticking to veggie juice with added vitamins?' she said. 'Or are you holding out for oatmeal?'

'You wish!' laughed Jack. 'I just prefer the blue ones.'

He grabbed his own tub of salty snacks and added a not-so-healthy heap to the side of his plate before tucking into the cheese board.

'Weirdo!' said Caroline.

It wasn't long before the pair of them had munched their way through their first helpings and were busy swapping bowls and passing boards of cold meat between them, loading up ready for a second innings.

It felt easy and relaxed… and Jack realised that he was suddenly feeling decidedly Christmassy. In fact, if this was the only moment of true celebration he had this year, it would still go down as the best Christmas he'd had in years.

'Hey, Caroline?' he said, leaning back in his chair and picking up his glass of wine.

'Yeah?' she said, grinning over at him.

'Toast?'

'Go on then,' she said, mirroring him.

'Thank you for making Christmas arrive early.'

'Aw,' she crooned. 'You cheesy sucker!'

Jack snorted in amusement. 'I'm serious, though. It's Christmas, and I tell the truth at Christmas.'

'Well, I'm having the best time too,' said Caroline, her smile easing into something more gentle. 'I know it sounds stupid, but I've been getting so stressed out about the blasted lights thing. It's been plaguing me so much that I've been wishing for Christmas to be over. But… you've reminded me how it's meant to feel.'

'Me and the several feet of snow outside?' said Jack.

'No. Just you.'

'That's the wine talking, Miss Cook,' said Jack.

'Nope, not the wine,' she said with a slow smile. 'Maybe the bath though… at least a little bit!'

'Well, that's fair enough,' said Jack with a shrug. 'It *is* quite an exceptional tub. I missed it while I was away.'

'I don't think I'd ever be able to leave it behind if it was mine,' said Caroline.

'Yeah… I know what you mean,' said Jack quietly. There was no way in the world he'd admit that he wasn't talking about the bathtub anymore. 'Anyway,' he said quickly, shaking his head and doing his best to undo the spell that seemed to have descended on him, 'the answer to your question—'

'What question?' said Caroline, sitting back with a little sigh.

'The question that's been plaguing you and causing you all that stress,' said Jack. 'The answer's yes. I'll turn on the Crumbleton Christmas lights for you… if you're sure you want me.'

'I do!' said Caroline with a little squeal. 'I want you!'

CHAPTER 11

CAROLINE

It was still relatively early in the evening, but Caroline could see that Jack's eyelids were getting heavy. Every blink had a bit of a delay, and he was struggling to keep up with the conversation too.

'Hey,' she said gently, as his head nodded right into the palm of his hand, 'I don't want to play mum or anything, but don't stay up on my account. Feel free to head to bed – I totally get it.'

'You sure?' said Jack, his voice a mumbled garble. 'I don't want you reporting the fact that I'm a lightweight who has the bedtime of a toddler!'

'I wouldn't dream of it,' said Caroline. 'Besides… I think if you leave it any longer, I'm going to have to carry you up the stairs. As much as I'm game for giving it a try, I'm not sure my insurance covers me carrying film stars to bed!'

'M'not film star,' murmured Jack. 'M'just Jack.'

'Alright, just Jack,' said Caroline, getting to her feet in the hope that he might follow suit. 'Whatever you are, you are *definitely* still jetlagged.'

'Can't argue, too tired,' yawned Jack, sliding to his feet just like she'd planned. 'What about you, though? I feel bad. I'm a rubbish host!'

'You're definitely not,' said Caroline. 'Anyway, don't worry about me, I can look after myself.'

'Okay,' yawned Jack, clearly too far gone to put up any kind of a fight. 'Help yourself to any of the spare bedrooms. Trish has got them all aired and the beds are made up. No idea why. It's always just me.'

Jack paused and a confused look crossed his face, as though he realised he'd just been super-vulnerable… but then he shrugged, clearly lacking the energy or brain space to worry about such things until the morning.

'It's all good,' said Caroline, taking pity on him. She almost wanted to gag the poor guy before he managed to blurt out anything more personal.

Caroline had already had a peep through the rest of the closed doors upstairs earlier on in the evening, and there was a clear winner…

'So… it's okay if I help myself to the epic four-poster, then?' she said lightly.

'Have at it!' he said with a sleepy smile. 'Wait – you haven't got PJs or anything. Need something to kip in?'

Caroline shook her head. She wasn't about to make

him run around after her in his state of half-snooziness.

'I'm fine,' she said.

She'd just sleep in her tee-shirt and undies and worry about the consequences in the morning. She was pretty sure she had her gym bag in the car – and that had a spare tee shirt and leggings in it. With any luck, she'd be able to sweep the snow off in the morning and grab it.

'By the way - thank you,' said Jack, trudging towards the door, looking very much like he was dragging his feet with every step.

'What on earth for?' said Caroline with a little laugh.

Goodness, he was even cuter when he was half-asleep!

'For getting stuck in the snow. And for staying. And for agreeing to marry me, of course!'

'My pleasure. All of it. I mean, I couldn't exactly turn you down considering you gave me this whopper!' she said, holding up her hand so that the giant plastic gem sparkled under the lights. 'Good night Jack, sweet dreams.'

Jack nodded sleepily. Then he opened his mouth to say something... paused... closed it again and promptly disappeared.

'Weirdest evening ever?' whispered Caroline to the empty room as she cocked her head and listened for Jack's soft footsteps making their way up the stairs.

As soon as she was sure he was safely on his way to

bed, Caroline made her way over towards the window. Twitching back the heavy curtains, she peeped out. The snow was still swirling in enthusiastic flurries, and it was hard to make out the beach. The moon wasn't anywhere to be seen – clearly tucked up behind the heavy blanket of clouds – but she could hear the waves lapping at the edges of the snowy beach.

With a little shiver, Caroline carefully closed the gap in the curtains. Then she turned to admire the Christmas tree. They really had done a brilliant job – despite their near-constant squabbling over the best bits of tinsel and the sparkliest ornaments. The lights twinkled at her, reflecting off the baubles and the giant star at the top.

Caroline grinned at the sight. Getting that star up there had nearly brought the entire tree down on their heads. Still – it had been worth it. In fact, she was starting to think it might be time to retire her tatty tinsel tree and treat herself to a real one.

'Maybe not, though,' she sighed. Because nothing was ever going to come close to decorating a seven-foot Christmas tree with her celebrity crush, was it?!

'You're in big trouble, my girl,' she muttered, turning her attention to the wood burner, which was still crackling away merrily.

A crush on Jack Jones had felt relatively safe when he'd been on the other side of the world – a random celebrity she was never likely to meet. He was just someone she could fantasise about at arm's length while tearing him to shreds in the newspaper – just to balance out all the mushy feelings she had in private. She'd never considered the chance that she might actually meet him one day.

Now… he was Jack. Not Jack Jones – film star. Just Jack. The funny guy who made ridiculous speeches when he got flustered, and fake-proposed with large, plastic rings. He was Jack, who let her borrow his bathtub and made sure she didn't just eat Pringles for tea. He was Jack – who went swimming with the snowflakes and smelled like a combination of cinnamon and saltwater.

Blowing out a long breath, Caroline tried to shake some sense into herself as she knelt down on the hearthrug. She'd quickly make sure that the fire was safe for the night, and then she'd head upstairs to her fancy-pants borrowed bed and go to sleep. With any luck, that would put a stop to all these dreamy hopes that seemed to be floating around in her head. She was under no illusions - there was only one place they could lead… disappointment.

But… well… she wasn't ready to turn in just yet. She was wired, and giddy, and ridiculously happy. She'd just spent the perfect evening with a lovely man… and she wasn't quite ready for the dream to come to an end. By the time the morning came, this would all be over. As soon as the snow melted, she'd have to head home.

'And then I might never see him again,' she sighed,

glancing down at her plastic engagement ring, still glimmering on her finger where he'd placed it.

Caroline swallowed as a wave of emotion rushed through her, and she let out a little sound that was somewhere between a laugh and a sob.

'Pull yourself together, woman!' she muttered, rolling her eyes at herself, even as she gave a great sniff.

Besides – she *would* see him again, wouldn't she?! Because, against all odds, Jack had said yes to her insane request. He was going to swoop in and save the day and turn on the Crumbleton Christmas lights. Or… turn them *back* on, she should say.

With a broad grin, Caroline opened the door of the wood burner. Instead of putting it to bed for the night, she added a large log from the stack on the hearth. She was going to make herself comfortable and re-live every single second of the best day she'd had in… hell, the best day she'd *ever* had!

Settling into the corner of the motheaten, cosy sofa, Caroline tucked her feet up underneath herself and let the warmth of the beautiful room wash over her. Then, realising that she didn't have to curl up into a tight ball like she did at home, she stretched her legs out luxuriously and snuggled even further into the cushions.

Turning to stare up at the ceiling, she watched as the fire threw swirling shadows across the plaster rose. She let out a long, happy sigh. The tide must be coming in beyond the windows because the sound of the waves seemed to be getting closer. The house was blissfully still, and the crackling fire was singing her a lullaby…

❋

Caroline woke with a start. She was lying under a heavy duvet that smelled… different. Turning over, she nearly hit the floor.

'What the…?!' she gasped, wrestling with a couple of cushions that had just tried to follow her.

Sitting up, she rubbed her eyes and peered around, trying to get her bearings.

Of course. She was at Jack's house… and she was still on his sofa.

'What a waste of a four-poster!' she yawned, cuddling the fluffy duvet to her chest.

The fire was still crackling away… but judging by the fact that daylight was creeping in around the edges of the curtains, she'd been asleep for hours.

If she was being honest, it was the best sleep she'd had in years – which was ridiculous, considering it had been on a tatty old sofa rather than between the Egyptian cotton sheets that had been waiting for her upstairs. Even so, her dreams had been full of glimmering plastic jewels, warm smiles, reading glasses, and the scent of saltwater and cinnamon.

As though she was still searching for the scent, Caroline sniffed the air. It was heavy with pine and…

'Coffee!' she whispered. Staring around for the

source of the deliciousness, she spotted a steaming mug on a little table just out of reach.

Jack had clearly been in while she'd been asleep - maybe more than once, judging by the lovely warm duvet, the still-steaming cup of coffee and the merry, dancing flames inside the wood burner.

Please tell me I wasn't snoring the house down?!

Caroline grabbed the cup of coffee and took a restorative sip. She sniffed the air again. It wasn't just coffee and the scent of the Christmas tree that tickled her nose. She could smell something wonderful... something that might mean... breakfast?

Jack Jones - celebrity... early bird... chef?

Scrambling to her feet, Caroline made her way over towards the window, clutching the coffee cup to her chest like a comfort blanket. Opening the heavy curtains just a crack, she peered out. At some point during the night, it had stopped snowing. The tide had reclaimed the beach and there was no sign of its snowy blanket from the night before.

Well... that had to be a good sign, didn't it? Either that or a really bad one. It depended on how you looked at it. On one hand, it meant that she had a good chance of getting back to Crumbleton if the roads had cleared as fast as the beach had, but on the other hand...

Caroline let out a long sigh. She couldn't help a little twinge of disappointment that it looked like this fantasy of hers was almost over.

If the roads *were* clear, there was nothing to keep her there.

Well… that being the case, she'd better go and find Jack to say thank you and goodbye.

Patting her hair with her free hand, Caroline gave her eyes a quick wipe on her cuff. It was about as much as she could do, considering she didn't have a mirror, a brush… or a makeup bag come to that!

'Right… time to return to reality, I guess,' she murmured.

Even if she didn't want to.

CHAPTER 12

JACK

'Did I wake you?' said Jack, turning to find Caroline standing in the doorway, watching him with wide, sleepy eyes.

'What time is it?' she yawned.

'Stupid o'clock,' said Jack with a sheepish smile. 'Sorry... my body clock is refusing to catch up – it's all over the place!'

'It wasn't you. I think it was the smell of coffee that did it.' Caroline yawned again and wandered over to the kitchen island, toasting him with her half-empty mug. 'Thank you. For future reference, that's definitely the best way to wake me up!'

'Noted,' said Jack, his stomach flipping in time with the pancake in the pan in front of him. The idea of doing this again with her in the future held more appeal than he'd ever imagined. 'Want a top-up?'

'Depends,' said Caroline.

'On what?' he said, his voice coming out all weird and husky.

'On what's in the pan,' she said with a sleepy smile. 'Because if it's what I'm hoping it is, I don't want you to get distracted.'

'Pancakes. I've got bacon and maple syrup,' he said, glancing at her over his shoulder only to see her crinkle her nose. 'Or, if you prefer, there are strawberries, chocolate chips, honey...'

'Now you're talking!' she said, her eyes twinkling at him.

'Excellent, more bacon for me!' he said with a broad smile, turning back to his pan before he really did cremate the pancake he was working on.

No one should look that cute after spending a night fully dressed on the sofa!

It had taken a ridiculous amount of self-control when he'd pottered downstairs in the middle of the night, only to find Caroline fast asleep in the living room. Jack had only left his bed because he'd spent a whole hour lying in the dark, staring at the ceiling as her mischievous smile danced in front of his eyes.

When he couldn't take it any longer, he'd hopped out of bed with the plan of adding another log to the wood burner so that it would still be going in the morning. Instead, he'd found her cuddled up in a chilly ball amongst the cushions.

Reigning in the temptation to run a finger across her cheek to brush the stray strands of hair away, Jack had hurried straight back upstairs and returned with a duvet. He'd draped it carefully over her, doing his best not to wake her in the process, and had then banked up the fire so that she wouldn't wake up stiff and cold to the bone in the morning.

He hadn't brushed her cheek. He hadn't kissed her forehead... but it *had* taken a ridiculous amount of willpower to dim the lights and walk out of that room.

'So... you're an early bird, huh?' she said, interrupting his slightly uncomfortable train of thought.

'It's partially the jetlag, and partially because of the last film I did,' said Jack, sliding another pancake onto the stack he was working on. 'I mean... I get up pretty early most of the time anyway, but this was a four a.m. start every day because of the makeup. It was brutal to start with, but I got used to it and now I can't get out of the habit.'

'I'm... *not* a morning person,' she shuddered. 'I think four a.m. starts would just about finish me off. I'd be a grumpy nightmare.'

'Uh-oh – also noted!' said Jack.

'Don't worry, you're safe,' she said.

'How come?' said Jack.

'Coffee and breakfast!' she said, as he turned and placed a stack of half a dozen perfect, golden pancakes in front of her and then pushed a bowl of strawberries and a bottle of honey towards her.

'Now you're talking!'

Jack grinned at her pure appreciation. It was ridiculously refreshing.

'You're definitely going down as the hostess with the mostest!' she said, drizzling honey all over her plate before taking a huge bite and letting out a loud groan of appreciation.

Jack's knees gave a treacherous tremble at the sound.

'I cleared the snow off your car,' he said, just for something to say. 'It didn't take long – it's just that soft, powdery stuff. It came off in a giant heap!'

'Oh – thank you,' she said, this time not taking her eyes off her breakfast.

'No worries. It looks like the road's been cleared too,' he said. 'I'm not sure how far they've got. Obviously, the drive is still covered. It shouldn't take me too long to clear it when you want to head off, though.'

Caroline shifted in her seat and Jack got the distinct impression that she wasn't quite sure how to react to this news. It made him weirdly happy that she wasn't already legging it through the door, desperate to return to reality.

He was… dreading it. He didn't actually want her to go. He wanted to spend the day laughing together. He could imagine Christmas shopping, making lunch… chatting about something and nothing…

'I'll get out of your hair as soon as possible, don't worry!' she said, cutting across his happy little fantasy.

Jack shook his head, his heart sinking. 'There's no rush – really!' he said. 'I'm enjoying your company.'

'Awww,' said Caroline, giving him a wide, sunny smile. 'Jack Jones, you old smoothy.'

'I'm serious,' said Jack. 'Just... don't make me regret it!'

Caroline snorted and Jack laughed as she managed to lose a bit of strawberry she'd been nibbling in the process.

'So,' she said, nodding at the script he'd left open on the kitchen island. 'What ya reading? Have you found the perfect project to dive into next?'

'What – to perfectly showcase my wooden abilities?' smirked Jack.

'Ah maaaan,' sighed Caroline. 'I'm sorry. Really. I never should have—'

'Only kidding,' laughed Jack. 'Actually, funny you should ask. I got a call from my agent in the middle of the night – just after I'd covered you up with that duvet, in fact.'

'Yeah – I meant to thank you for that,' said Caroline.

Jack grinned at her. 'My pleasure.'

'So... what did your agent want?' said Caroline, clearly intrigued. In fact, Jack had a feeling it was costing her a great deal of effort not to slip into reporter-mode and start bombarding him with questions.

'Well,' he said slowly, 'I've been offered a new role.'

'Congratulations!' said Caroline.

'Thanks,' said Jack. 'Aimee – that's my agent – she's really excited about it. That's why she called at such an ungodly hour. She said it's one of those "career-defining roles" – and she wants an answer asap.'

'Wow,' said Caroline. 'That's cool!'

'It is,' said Jack slowly. 'It's the lead role… the start of a huge franchise. I mean…' he trailed off and ran his fingers through his hair.

It really was mind-blowing that he'd been offered the role. A big compliment – and an even bigger opportunity. So *why* did it feel like saying yes would be some kind of cosmic mistake?

No – making a huge, life-changing decision based on a woman he'd met less than twenty-four hours ago would be a cosmic mistake!

'You don't look very happy about it,' said Caroline, raising her eyebrows curiously.

'I guess I'm still processing it all,' said Jack.

'Why don't you tell me about it?' said Caroline. 'It might help it feel more real!'

'Okay – good idea,' said Jack, nodding slowly. 'So, it's got a pretty huge budget. It's the start of a franchise, so it could mean years of work for me. I've not actually read the whole script yet, but—'

'Wait, if you've not read it yet, how come they've offered…' Caroline trailed off.

'The writers had me in mind from the start, apparently,' said Jack, rubbing his neck and feeling decidedly awkward. He didn't like to brag, but this really *was* a big deal.

'Um, wow!' said Caroline. 'That's seriously amazing.'

'Yeah.' Jack shrugged. 'Huge jump in earnings, amazing script according to Aimee…'

'What am I not getting about all this?' said Caroline. 'You don't seem to be very excited!'

'It's shooting in New Zealand,' said Jack. 'I'd be away for at least eight months… probably more. If the franchise really took off… well, I'd barely be here.'

'Oh,' said Caroline.

Jack watched as she put her fork down, a chunk of strawberry and honey-drizzled pancake still attached to its prongs. The pair of them sat in silence for a long moment.

'So…' said Caroline, finally turning to meet his eye, 'when do you have to leave?'

'I've not given them my answer yet,' said Jack in a small voice.

'You… you haven't?' gasped Caroline, surprise written all over her face.

Jack stared at her. As much as he wanted to, he couldn't tell Caroline it was because he couldn't bear the thought of being on the other side of the planet… when she was here.

'I… erm… I'm not sure it's quite the right vehicle for me,' he said, making up an excuse on the spot.

'You're such an *actor!*' she laughed. 'But... I guess that's fair enough – if that's the way you feel.'

'Not sure Aimee will let me off the hook quite so easily,' he sighed.

'I bet,' said Caroline. 'Hey - is that the script for it?' She nodded with interest at the bound document Jack had been reading when she'd entered the room.

Jack shook his head. 'That's one of the ones from the bookshelf.'

'Oh!' said Caroline, looking more than a little bit confused. 'Are you considering doing that one instead?'

'Hell no!' he laughed.

'Why not?'

'Because it's an animation about a talking dog in space,' said Jack.

'Sooo... why are you reading it?' said Caroline, picking her fork back up.

'I just like the story!' said Jack with a grin.

CHAPTER 13

CAROLINE

'*You* stayed *where?!*' gasped Milly.

She was busy tying a bunch of red roses dotted with festive berries and frothy white gypsophila. Right now, though, the ribbon was dangling loosely from her fingers, and the blooms were in serious danger of landing on the shop floor.

'…and with *who?!*' she added, her voice shrill.

'Shhhh!' laughed Caroline, shooting a look towards the door. Luckily Jo – Milly's decidedly nosy assistant – hadn't returned from the coffee run Milly had sent her on the minute Caroline had dropped the code word for "have gossip".

'Sorry,' muttered Milly. 'It's fine… she won't be back for a few more minutes.'

'Good,' said Caroline. 'As I was saying – I stayed at Crumbleton Sands with Jack Jones.'

'*The* Jack Jones?' said Milly.

'The one and only,' said Caroline, doing her best not to look too smug.

'The one you called Captain Woodentop in your last film review?' said Milly, raising an eyebrow.

It really was decidedly inconvenient having friends who read every single word you wrote – especially when they quoted the annoying bits back at you!

'Yes. And... I *may* have been a bit harsh,' she conceded.

'Caroline Cook, you're blushing,' gasped Milly.

'Am not,' muttered Caroline, mentally cursing the flush that was spreading over her cheeks.

'Ooh, this is getting interesting,' said Milly. 'And you only managed to drive back this morning?!'

'Yep,' said Caroline. 'And for the record, it was horrible! The marshes were a slushy nightmare, but I swear the worst part was walking up the high street. Andy's not back, and whoever they've got covering for him hasn't finished gritting the cobbles yet – it's lethal out there!'

'That's an understatement,' said Milly. 'I bet it was terrifying in your little car - the only reason I managed to get in is because of Murray's four-by-four.'

'Ah, the joys of shacking up with the marsh ranger!' said Caroline.

'Enough about him,' said Milly, waving a dismissive hand. 'I want to hear all about your night with a movie star!'

'Again – SHHHH!' said Caroline.

'Caroline and Ja-a-ck sitting in a tree... K-I-S-S—'

'Nope. There was none of that!' said Caroline, cutting her off quickly. 'He was a perfect gentleman. Plus, he's still completely jetlagged so he disappeared to bed at toddler o'clock, leaving me to fall asleep on the sofa.'

'I can't believe he didn't have the good manners to offer you his bed!' said Milly.

'Dude – he offered me a four-poster of my own,' said Caroline. 'I just never made it upstairs. I fell asleep in front of the fire, and then he covered me up with a duvet in the middle of the night so that I didn't get cold.'

'So romantic!' sighed Milly, clutching the roses to her chest.

Caroline desperately wanted to agree and let out a soppy little sigh of her own... but she didn't dare. She was already regretting the fact that she'd told Milly this much. She knew she should stop... but she had to tell someone before she burst!

'Not romantic,' said Caroline, lying through her teeth. 'Practical and... kind.'

'What I want to know is what you were doing there in the first place?' demanded Milly. 'Were you working on a story? Some kind of festive fix-up?!'

'As if I would!' said Caroline. 'And you have to promise not to spill the beans if I tell you.'

'You know I won't,' said Milly impatiently. 'Hurry up before Jo gets back!'

'Okay, okay... so I've found our special guest for the Crumbleton Christmas lights,' said Caroline.

'That's epic! Only you could rustle up a film star when you couldn't find anyone else,' said Milly. Then she started to giggle. 'Shame you had to spend the night to convince him, though!'

'Spend the night with who?' said Jo, appearing in the doorway with a tray of coffees clutched in her hands.

Caroline winced and widened her eyes at Milly. She could swear Jo had the hearing of a bat – which was a complete nightmare when combined with Milly's excitable exclamations.

'No one!' said Milly, doing her best to sound innocent.

Caroline shook her head furiously. If Jo cottoned on to the fact that they were talking about Jack, it would be all over Crumbleton by lunchtime.

'Fine, be like that,' said Jo, plonking the coffees down in front of them and wandering through to the back room, clearly deciding that it couldn't be very interesting anyway.

Caroline let out a long, low sigh of relief.

'Sorry!' Milly mouthed. 'So...' she said at normal volume, clearly looking for a way to continue the conversation in code. 'Was there any kind of... erm... *payment* for the appearance?' She wiggled her eyebrows suggestively.

'No!' said Caroline, rolling her eyes and shaking her

head. 'It was completely voluntary... though it took a while to get the go-ahead.'

'Like... he needed to sleep on it?' said Milly, her eyebrows going into overdrive.

'Something like that,' said Caroline. 'But *not* like that!'

'And what was the... erm... property you viewed like?' said Milly. 'Soulless holiday home?'

Caroline shook her head again. She felt awful about saying that, now that she knew how much the place meant to Jack and the fact that he seemed pretty keen on turning it into a proper home.

If he didn't end up disappearing off to New Zealand, of course.

Caroline pushed the thought to the back of her mind.

'It's really... cosy,' she said at last. 'I helped decorate the Christmas tree while I was there.'

'Awwww' said Milly, her voice rising in an excitable squeak as she squashed the flowers even further.

'Oi!' hissed Caroline, a warning note to her voice.

'What?' said Milly innocently. 'It's just nice to see you so happy.'

'Who said I'm happy?' demanded Caroline.

'Your stupid smiley face!' chuckled Milly.

'Fine,' huffed Caroline. 'It *was* nice. Kind of... ordinary, you know?'

'Ooh, I do!' said Milly.

'Nothing ordinary about his bathtub though!' she added.

'I *knew* there had to be more to this!' said Milly, looking thrilled.

'More to what?' said Jo, wandering through from the back room, and staring at the ruined flowers clutched to her boss's chest.

'Oh… to the Christmas lights switch on,' said Milly quickly, popping the battered bouquet down onto the table and turning an easy smile on Jo.

'Right…?' said Caroline, hoping Jo wasn't about to latch onto that surprising snippet.

'Like what?' said Jo, looking half interested.

'Liiike…' Milly raised an eyebrow at Caroline, clearly passing the baton.

Damnit!

'Like… it's going to happen the night before Christmas Eve,' said Caroline quickly.

'Uh-huh?' said Jo, looking less than impressed. 'I mean… you've moved the date like three times already, so that's not exactly news.'

'Yeah – but it's going to be bigger and better than ever!' said Milly.

Caroline gave her head a quick shake. Milly bit her lip looking guilty, and Caroline rolled her eyes. Maybe Jo wasn't the one she should be worrying about after all.

'How so?' said Jo.

'A market!' said Caroline, quickly making

something up on the spot. 'We're going to have stalls. Hot chocolate, carol singing, last-minute pressies.'

'That's… actually, that's a really nice idea,' said Jo grudgingly.

'Yeah, it totally is!' said Milly with a sly smile.

'That's why I'm here,' said Caroline, deciding she had no choice but to run with it. 'To make sure the shop will be open – and that you two are up for it.'

'I'm in,' said Jo. 'As long as I get the chance to do some shopping too.'

'I guess I can't really say no!' said Milly.

Caroline grinned at her. 'Nope, you really can't!'

Tough!

If her friend had been planning a relaxed evening being all loved-up with Murray, she should have kept her mouth shut and not forced Caroline to make up something so ridiculous on the spot.

Then again… it *wasn't* so ridiculous, was it?

Jack had said he wanted to start meeting people in a low-key way. He could turn the lights on and then she could quietly introduce him to a few people. A bit of a last-minute shopping event along with carols and hot chocolate would help take the spotlight off him a little bit. As long as she didn't announce his presence in advance, he should be fairly safe from any press… other than her, of course!

'So… who's the special guest going to be?' said Jo.

'It's a surprise,' said Caroline quickly, before Milly could put her foot in it again.

'That means you still don't have anyone, doesn't it?' laughed Jo.

'Worst case scenario, you can do it Jo!' said Milly.

'Always nice to be bottom of the pile,' huffed Jo, heading over to tidy up the shelves bearing her Grumpy Plant collection.

'So,' said Milly, sidling up to Caroline so that she could whisper right in her ear.

'So what?' said hissed Caroline.

'So - you *like him* like him, don't you?'

Caroline shivered as Milly's warm breath hit her ear. She bit her lip, not saying anything.

'You're not starstruck, are you?' demanded Milly.

Caroline eyeballed Milly and shook her head.

'Wait… was that a "no" to question number one or number two?' said Milly. 'No, you don't *like* him, or no, you're not starstruck?!'

'You'll just have to wait and see!' said Caroline with a grin.

'Aww, tell me!' said Milly.

Caroline shook her head again. 'Thanks to you, I've got an event to plan… must dash!'

CHAPTER 14

JACK

'Well, this is a turn-up for the books!' said Brian, shooting Jack an intrigued look as he clambered into the front passenger seat of the taxi. 'Who'd have thought you'd fancy coming to Crumbleton when everyone in town's going to be out and about?!'

'Well... it *is* Christmas,' said Jack vaguely. 'I fancied a bit of company.'

'Rubbish,' said Brian, catching his eye and giving him a penetrating look. 'There's something else going on, isn't there?!'

Jack grinned. It was basically impossible to keep a secret from Brian, and now that he was on the way to Crumbleton for the big event at last, he couldn't really see any reason not to come clean.

'It's like this,' said Jack, 'I simply can't miss the big switch-on of the Christmas lights.'

'Lad, I hope you haven't been getting too excited,' chuckled Brian. 'I mean, all that happens is someone flips the switch off, and someone else flips it back on again.'

'Yep, I know,' said Jack. 'Because I just happen to be the "someone else" in that scenario.'

'What? You aren't... are you?' gasped Brian. 'You're the top-secret special guest?'

'Yep, I am,' he laughed.

'You just wait until I tell Trish!' said Brian. 'She'll be *that* proud. So... I'm guessing Caroline Cook got to you and turned the thumb screws then?'

'Something like that,' chuckled Jack, staring straight ahead in case his friend spotted the excitement in his eyes at the sound of her name.

Jack had practically driven himself to distraction over the past few days. Ever since Caroline had left the morning after the snowstorm, he hadn't been able to sit still. He'd wanted to call her... to visit her in Crumbleton... to spend time with her...

He'd felt like a teenager, hovering over his phone, waiting for Caroline to call with the promised details of the Crumbleton Christmas Lights event.

To stop himself from making an epic prat out himself, Jack had upped his number of daily sea swims to keep himself busy - but even those hadn't been enough to keep the bubbly, bouncy ray of sunshine out of his head for long.

'Mind you,' said Brian, dragging Jack's attention

back to the present, 'this does mean our efforts have been wasted.'

'What efforts?' said Jack, blinking as he did his best to catch up with the conversation.

'Me – dashing around, keeping your presence quiet,' laughed Brian. 'Poor Trish – I still don't think she quite believes it, even though she's been working for you for more than a year.'

Jack laughed. 'Well… just to say – your efforts weren't wasted. At all.'

'I was just pulling your leg, boy,' said Brian, shooting him a warm smile.

'I know, but I'm serious,' said Jack. 'Thank you, Brian, for all your friendship. I don't know what I'd have done without your help. Trish's too.'

'Oh, good lord, you're going all soppy on me,' said Brian. 'I wish you wouldn't when I'm driving and can't give you a hug!'

'Now who's a softy?!' laughed Jack.

'Takes one to know one, boy,' said Brian seriously. 'But… you're welcome. We're always glad to help.'

'You and Trish have been my safe space whenever I've come home – and there aren't many people I can say that about.'

'Quit it, or you'll make me cry,' huffed Brian. 'And then I won't be able to focus on my darts.'

'Okay, fine,' said Jack. 'But I owe you. I'll find a way to repay you both for your kindness one day.'

'Well,' said Brian, 'that's easy enough. You can pay us both back this evening.'

'Oh yeah?' said Jack, suddenly feeling slightly uneasy. Was his friend about to ask him to sign his wife's butt cheeks or something? It wouldn't be the first time he'd endured that request... but it would *definitely* be a bit more awkward, given the small-town setting.

'Yeah,' said Brian. 'I can't get no blighter to come and join me for darts later tonight. Ruby's busy with her book deadline, and I think Oli's making sure she stops to eat and drink occasionally.'

'Darts?' said Jack.

'I'd consider it a great favour,' said Brian. 'Besides, if you want to get the locals on-side, a trip to the Dolphin and Anchor is a good plan anyway.'

'Hey – no need for the made-up reasons,' chuckled Jack, 'I'd love a game. Does... erm... does Caroline ever play?'

'Caroline Cook?' said Brian, his beady eyes snapping to Jack – who instantly wanted to kick himself.

'Yes.'

'The one who's somehow – mysteriously – managed to talk you out of your hidey-hole tonight to do her a favour?' said Brian.

'Yes.'

'The one who hates your guts?!' he added with a wicked gleam in his eye.

'That's the one,' laughed Jack.

'Yes, she does sometimes,' he said. 'Though if you're planning on picking a fight with her, would you mind leaving it till after we've had a few games?'

'I reckon I can manage that,' said Jack with a grin. 'Hey – you said something about repaying Trish too…?'

'Yeah,' said Brian. 'She's one of the carollers, and they're always looking for more men. Unfortunately, I can't help because I sound like a squashed frog. Any chance you'd be up for a few carols?'

'Ah,' said Jack. 'Well… yes. Of course. In fact, I've already been roped in!'

'That's wonderful!' said Brian. 'Well, you're full of surprises tonight. Trish is going to be chuffed.'

'We'll see,' she Jack. 'She hasn't heard me sing yet!'

But apparently, Caroline had. When she'd called him to fill him in on the finer details of the event, she'd not-so-subtly dropped the bombshell that she'd heard him singing in the shower. Then, she'd promptly begged him to join in with the carollers for at least one song. Jack had been so happy to hear her voice again that he'd agreed to it before he'd realised what he was doing.

'Well, I have to say, you're probably the most exciting guest we've ever had for the lights switch on,' said Brian. 'Of course, it's bigger and better than ever this year.'

'Mmm,' said Jack. He wasn't entirely sure how to feel about the fact that the event had mushroomed into an entire Christmas market, complete with mulled wine and hot chocolate stalls as well as the carol singing.

Part of him – his inner excited four-year-old who couldn't wait for Christmas – was thrilled, but the part of him that had been so concerned about maintaining his privacy and not ramming his presence down the locals' throats was dreading it. Luckily, there was a third part in play – the one that simply couldn't say no to Caroline Cook.

'So... if you wouldn't mind dropping me up near the museum, that'd be grand,' said Jack as they neared the City Gates, and his stomach flipped with a mixture of excitement and pure fear.

'You're kidding, right?' said Brian, his voice serious.

'Erm... no...' said Jack.

'Sorry mate, but this sleigh doesn't actually fly. The high street's been officially closed to all traffic, barring emergency vehicles, since lunchtime to give all the stallholders time to set up!'

'And... the museum's at the top of town,' said Jack, nodding slowly.

'Yep – still where it was when you were a nipper,' said Brian. 'Quite a stretch, but nothing I can do about it tonight, sadly. Anyway... it's not like there's any point in you trying to hide, is there? You'll be the focus of everyone's attention in about an hour anyway!'

Jack nodded even as his knees quaked. This was ridiculous. He'd spent years dealing with the press – he was used to having cameras shoved in his face, both the movie kind *and* the paparazzi kind. He was pretty sure he could handle an evening hanging out with a tiny crowd of locals.

'You look like you've just seen a ghost,' chuckled Brian. 'They won't bite, I promise!'

'I'm okay,' said Jack, forcing a smile.

'You'll be grand, lad,' said Brian. 'Tell you what, I might have something in the back seat you can use as a bit of a disguise. Plus, I'll walk up to the top of town with you. We can go up the back steps so you don't get mobbed.'

'What about your darts?' said Jack.

'Can't start without you!' said Brian. 'Besides, you might need a bodyguard.'

'I thought you said the locals don't bite?' said Jack, alarmed.

'They don't… but Caroline Cook might!'

Jack snorted.

'I'm sure I can handle her,' he said, unable to keep the broad grin off his face.

In fact, he couldn't wait to see her. Jack had some news to share with Caroline Cook… he just hoped she was as excited about it as he was.

CHAPTER 15

CAROLINE

Caroline was buzzing. The entire town had come out to play. Considering she'd only announced the event a couple of days ago and no one other than Milly knew who her super-special guest was – she had to say, she was chuffed.

The only grumble she'd received was from Geraldine in the antiques shop – and that was only because she'd had such a busy lead-up to Christmas already, she was concerned she didn't have enough trinkets to fill her stall with last-minute gift options. Caroline had simply herded the woman back inside her cave of a shop. Within five minutes, she'd helped to gather enough jewellery, vintage baubles and other assorted white elephants to fill not just one but three tables.

Every single shopkeeper in Crumbleton had agreed

to join in the fun – as long as the weather held – and at last, the weather gods had been in Caroline's favour. They'd been blessed with a chilly but clear night. Somewhere, far above the gleaming Christmas lights, Caroline knew the stars were peeping through the darkness of the December night sky.

'I'm loving this!' called Milly, as Caroline ambled towards her little stall at the top of the hill.

'Isn't it cool?' said Caroline, her eyes scanning the crowd, watching as everyone's breath plumed in the frozen air.

Crumbleton's residents were already out in force, milling up and down the cobbles, sipping hot chocolate or mulled wine, and buying all sorts of knickknacks as they went. But Caroline wasn't focussing on the usual suspects. She was looking for someone else - one face in particular – one that everyone here would know the minute they spotted him.

The weird thing was, Caroline felt like she'd been keeping an eye out for Jack all week – which was completely ridiculous. She knew for a fact that he wouldn't dare to venture into town before he had to. Still, ever since her unexpected sleepover at his place, Caroline had lived in a strange little bubble of hope that he might turn up in her office, or that she might spot him in the aisles of Bendall's.

No such luck.

There was something bittersweet about the fact that she'd fallen a little bit in love with her celebrity crush.

Or – a lot a bit!

But… she couldn't let herself think like that, could she? The man in question was due to turn up at any moment to do the honours with the Christmas lights… but then he'd be gone… and not just back to Crumbleton Sands.

Caroline sighed. She had no doubt that Jack would see sense about the role he'd been offered in that new movie franchise. His agent would make sure of it. He'd be on his way to New Zealand before she knew it… winging his way out of her life.

Caroline wasn't delusional enough to think that their little interlude had meant as much to him as it had to her. It was just a strange bit of Christmas magic - something she'd always hold close to her heart, even if it barely registered as a blip on Jack's radar.

'Your man not here yet?' said Milly, lowering her voice.

Caroline shook her head. 'Shhh!' she said automatically.

Milly giggled, adjusting a couple of the stunning wreaths she'd whipped up for her stall.

'I think the cat'll be out of the bag in a few minutes, anyway,' said Milly, 'given that the poor bloke is going to have to make his way up the high street through this lot! Did you even tell him about the back steps?'

'I… oh!' Caroline pulled a face. 'I didn't think to.'

'Meany!' chuckled Milly.

The reality was, Caroline had been so excited to

have an excuse to speak to Jack when she'd called to fill him in on the details of the event, she'd ended up getting strangely tongue-tied... something Jack had found ridiculously funny.

Caroline had promptly paid him back by roping him into join the carollers for at least a couple of songs. In fact... they'd just been settling back into their easy banter when Jack received another call – this time from his agent. One hurried apology later and the line had gone dead.

'Earth to Caroline?!' said Milly.

Caroline gave herself a little shake. 'Huh?'

'Hadn't you better stop mooning around and go down to the Gates to rescue the poor guy?'

'Erm... actually, good plan,' said Caroline, glancing at her watch. 'Though I might be a bit late for that...'

'Yep, you are!'

The deep voice behind her made Caroline whip around. She came face to face with Brian Singer, who was wearing a seriously cute jumper with a stuffed figgy pudding right over his belly.

'Brian!' she said with a broad smile. Then she frowned. That hadn't been Brian's voice.

Caroline glanced at the tall figure next to the friendly cabby and let out a loud hoot of laughter.

'What on earth are you wearing, Mr Film Star?!'

'Shhh!' growled Brian, shooting a furtive look around them. 'You're spoiling his disguise!'

Jack didn't seem to mind though, as he was

grinning down at her from beneath a towering Christmas tree bonnet. Layer upon green layer of stuffed crochet, complete with coloured baubles added about a foot to his height.

'Told you it's a rubbish disguise!' he laughed.

'Well, it's all I had in the cab,' huffed Brian. 'Other than the reindeer headband.'

Jack nodded and pulled option b out of his coat pocket. Before Caroline knew what was happening, he reached out, brushed her hair back off her face with gentle fingers, and popped the felt antlers on her head.

'Tell me I look as cute wearing my disguise as you do right now,' he said, grinning down at her.

Caroline swallowed. A Christmas miracle seemed to have just happened – she'd lost the use of her voice.

'Sorry mate, but nope,' laughed Milly. 'Yours just looks like a big, green, woolly arrow pointing right at your head!'

Jack snorted.

'So... you recognise him?' said Brian.

'Of course!' said Milly, rolling her eyes. 'I mean, it's not like I'm going to miss it when Ryan Reynolds rocks up to my market stall, is it?'

'Told you it worked,' said Brian, looking smug.

'I'm not sure that counts!' laughed Jack. 'Can I take it off now please?'

'Aw,' said Caroline, finding her voice again – though it was decidedly husky. 'Why don't you want to stand in front of Crumbleton with a Christmas tree on your head?'

'What can I say,' laughed Jack, 'I'm a total diva!'

'Yeah, you are,' said Caroline with a grin.

She was having a hard time stopping herself from reaching out and wrapping her arms around the man. She could still feel a light tingling on her cheeks where he'd touched her – like tiny traces of magic were at work on her skin. He was… delicious. No one should look that cute in a crotchet Christmas tree hat!

Blimey!

She needed to get things rolling, otherwise she was going to do something stupid right in front of the entire town.

'Right… are you ready for it?' she said, doing her best to pull herself together.

'As ready as I'll ever be,' said Jack. 'Nice to meet you, Milly.'

'You too, Ryan!' said Milly with a grin.

'Oh… can you reserve that wreath for me, please?' he added quickly, pointing at a large one dotted with tiny red roses and pinecones. 'And one of those potted Venus Flytraps too?'

'You've got it!' said Milly, looking thrilled.

'Okay,' said Jack, sounding nervous. 'Let's get this over with.'

'Yeah – then you can make a start on the carolling!' said Caroline.

'Damnit, I thought you'd forgotten about that!' huffed Jack.

'He didn't,' said Brian as Caroline took Jack's hand and started towing him through the gathering crowd towards the little podium she'd set up outside the museum. 'In fact, he told me he's looking forward to it.'

'Traitor!' huffed Jack, and Caroline saw him shoot a wink at Brian before he was swallowed up by the crowd.

'Right, let's do this,' she said, leading Jack towards the stage. She rather liked the feel of his large, warm hand in hers... so much so that she didn't want to let it go. But considering they were about to have the attention of the entire town on them, she thought it might be for the best.

'Aw,' said Jack as their fingers parted. 'I was kind of hoping you were going to hold my hand through the whole thing.'

'Baby,' she chuckled.

'Nope – you're just lovely and warm,' said Jack.

Caroline had a hard time tearing her eyes away from his smile... and for a moment she wished they were standing somewhere a little bit less conspicuous than on the makeshift stage in front of dozens of people who'd known her since she was in nappies.

'Alright!' she yelled, breaking the spell and making Jack jump in the process.

Heads turned towards them. Here and there, Caroline caught little gasps as the locals started to recognise the special guest she'd managed to rustle up for the big occasion.

She grabbed the large, brass handbell she'd left next to the microphone stand, and gave it a hefty shake. The ringing echoed down the high street, booming through several strategically placed speakers.

'Who's ready for our Christmas lights?' she shouted.

There was a loud cheer, and the crowd in front of the stage thickened as more people joined them.

'I've got a very special guest for you this year,' she said, shooting a smile at Jack. He looked very much like he'd quite like to disappear through the platform. 'I am thrilled to welcome Jack Jones to Crumbleton!'

'Who?' yelled a voice from the crowd. It sounded suspiciously like Brian Singer.

Everyone erupted with laughter, and Caroline saw Jack grinning back at them – the ice well and truly thawed.

'So!' said Caroline, glancing back into the darkness inside the museum, 'are my little elves back there ready?'

She got a disembodied thumbs-up from Harold Pottinger, who'd been loitering inside, waiting for her to give the sign. Suddenly, the street was plunged into gloom as the lights were turned off. There was a collective *"awwww"* of disappointment from the crowd.

'Ready for your big moment?' muttered Caroline with her hand over the microphone, as she handed Jack a comically large light switch that had a lead trailing from it.

'Ready,' he said, taking hold of it.

'Three!' yelled Caroline into the microphone.

'Two!' cheered the crowd.

'One!' Jack shouted into the microphone, flipping the switch.

A massive cheer went up as light flooded the street again, golden and twinkling on the happy faces below as they all raised their cups of mulled wine and hot chocolate in celebration.

'Speech!' yelled someone.

Caroline peered out at the crowd and saw the culprit grinning back at her. It was Milly.

Jack shot her a look, and she nodded encouragingly.

'Merry Christmas, Crumbleton.' He paused while everyone cheered. 'Thank you for letting me share this evening with you.'

As he continued to talk, Caroline realised she had her eyes fixed on his face. She wasn't listening to what he was saying… just soaking in the way he was saying it. His face was alive, and his eyes were full of fun as he held the crowd in the palm of his hand.

Caroline swallowed and did her best to tear her gaze off him, before everyone in town managed to clock the adoring look that was probably plastered across her face right now.

'There's not much more to say,' said Jack, surprising

her out of her daze by grabbing her hand and giving it a squeeze. 'Other than – enjoy!'

The crowd cheered again, and Jack stepped back from the microphone.

'Nice job,' said Caroline with a smile.

'Ta,' he said, leaning in close and kissing her cheek.

It took a few moments before Caroline realised that the simple kiss had just earned a bigger cheer than the Christmas lights.

CHAPTER 16

JACK

'Here you go, my boy, get that down you,' said Brian, placing a pint of black, velvety Guinness down in front of Jack. 'I'm betting you'll need something to whet your whistle after all that singing!'

'You're not wrong there, cheers!' said Jack, lifting the glass and taking a deep gulp.

The carolling had been far more fun than he'd expected. Instead of bowing out after a couple of token songs, he'd stayed with the little group until they were finished.

Jack had to hand it to them all, they had brilliant poker faces. Far from making a fuss about him joining them, he'd only received one or two astonished glances the first time he'd opened his mouth and his deep baritone had joined the other voices. After that, they just seemed to accept him as one of their own.

The collecting tin they'd had with them had filled up nicely, and they'd had to swap to a borrowed bucket from Milly's flower stall in the end.

'Right, let's get this party started!' said Brian excitedly, heading over to the dartboard and wiping off the old chalk scores with a rag.

Jack watched in amusement as the people standing close by hurriedly shuffled out of the way, leaving a nice clear bit of space around the board... no mean feat considering the fact that the Dolphin and Anchor was packed to the gunnels!

'Heads up,' said Jack, 'you should probably know that I'm better at carols than darts – and that's not saying much!'

'Good,' said Brian with a broad smile. 'I like a nice, easy win, so not to worry. Besides, I'm sure you've had plenty of practice. Bet you're a bit of a ringer...'

'I'm really not!' said Jack. 'I mean. Other than a few games when I was a teenager, I think the closest I've come since is throwing a few rubber-tipped spears in a film.'

'I don't remember that one...?' said Brian.

'Mmm,' said Jack. 'Not surprised, it went straight to DVD – and my scene got cut!'

'Too bad,' said Brian.

'Not really - I was rubbish!'

'Well, let's see how you get on, shall we?' said Brian cheerfully, holding out the darts to him.

Jack took them and glanced around. No one was

paying him the slightest bit of attention... and he loved it! His eyes landed on Caroline. She was perched on a stool by the bar, deep in conversation with the woman who owned the bakery... Helen... Hannah...? He wracked his brain, trying to remember her name. He'd met so many people over the last few hours that his head was spinning with them all.

'Don't worry, your date's still happy over there with Heather,' laughed Brian.

Heather – that was it!

'Not my date,' said Jack.

Sadly.

He still couldn't tear his eyes away from Caroline, though. She'd taken off her big, puffy coat and was wearing a sparkly red dress. She still had her antlers on too...

'Earth to Jack?' said Brian. 'Focus boy, or you're going to have someone's eye out. These darts don't actually have rubber tips, you know!'

'Right, right...' said Jack vaguely, turning towards the board and hurling a dart at it without much thought.

Brian sniggered. 'Okay, I stand corrected, you're definitely not a ringer!' He chalked up a great big number one on the board with a decided amount of glee.

Jack reined in the temptation to stick his tongue out at his friend – which was almost as strong as the temptation to look over at Caroline again.

Throw the dart, idiot!

'Nine!' said Brian. 'Bit better…'

Jack celebrated with a glance at Caroline. She was still nattering away – now to the young girl behind the bar. He caught the gleam of a yellow plastic gem as she reached for her glass of wine. She was still wearing the ring!

Grinning and feeling more cheerful than was probably normal about a tacky plastic ring, Jack hurled his final dart. It went wide and bounced off the protective foam layer surrounding the board.

'And that's a big fat zero,' laughed Brian.

Jack laughed and took a swig of his drink as he watched Brian score three beauties in quick succession.

'You're up!' said Brian.

'Mind if I team up with someone?' said Jack, as Brian jotted down his score. 'Just so that I stand a tiny chance here!'

'Go for it,' said Brian. 'The more the merrier.'

Jack hurried towards the bar and reached Caroline's side just as a couple approached her. There was something strangely dazed looking about the woman.

'Wow, you've left your laptop!' said Caroline, leaning in to give the woman a hug.

'That's because she's finished,' said the man, proudly. 'And she wouldn't rest until she'd come out to support you.'

'Finished?' said Jack, staring at the pair. He was sure

he hadn't seen them out and about during the festivities, and yet the woman looked familiar…

'Sorry, where are my manners?!' laughed Caroline. 'Jack, this is Oli and—'

'Oh my god!' gasped Jack, cutting across her. 'You're Ruby Hutchinson! I'm a huge fan!'

He knew his voice had gone all high and squeaky, but right now he didn't care. His favourite writer was standing right in front of him.

'Can I have your autograph?' he gasped. 'Caroline, have you got a pen? Damn… I haven't got any paper. Maybe I can get some from behind the bar…?'

'Dork!' chuckled Caroline.

'Wait,' said Ruby, blinking sleepily as she stared from Jack to Caroline, and then up at Oli, 'am I hallucinating? I know I'm tired and a bit out of it… but is Jack Jones asking me for my autograph right now?'

'Yep,' laughed Oli, 'he is. You've not *completely* lost it.'

'But… why's Jack Jones here?' she said, blinking in confusion.

'He's here with Caroline,' said Oli. 'At least… I think he is?'

Jack answered with a tiny nod, and Caroline beamed at him.

'How long was I writing that damn book?' said Ruby, looking completely lost.

Oli grinned as Ruby frowned. Then she gave a little shrug and nestled her head against Oli's shoulder, clearly half asleep.

'Don't worry, man,' said Oli, reaching out to shake Jack's hand. 'I'll make sure we sort that out for you… but maybe after she's had some sleep.'

Caroline patted Ruby on the head and Jack gave them a little wave as Oli drew Ruby away – presumably back home so that she could get some much-needed rest.

'Wow,' said Jack shaking his head. 'I can't believe I got to meet her!'

'Total fanboy!' laughed Caroline. 'So – have you finished your game with Brian?'

'No… that's why I came over!' said Jack, suddenly remembering that he'd abandoned his friend mid-game. 'I need help!'

'Brian giving you a hard time?' said Caroline.

'Something like that,' said Jack, not wanting to admit that it was actually the sight of her in her beautiful dress and antlers that had him on the back foot. 'Pretty please come over and be on my team?'

'Let me at him!' said Caroline, hopping off her stool and grabbing Jack's hand so that he could lead the way through the crowded bar back to Brian.

At the feel of her warm hand wrapped safely in his, Jack promptly lost the power of speech… but that didn't matter.

'Here we go!' said Caroline, as Brian handed her the darts, a look of amused surprise on his face that she was Jack's chosen teammate.

Caroline threw the three darts in quick succession.

'Well,' said Brian, his eyebrows shooting up. 'There's our ringer! Fifty-three. My goodness, you've been hiding your light under a bushel, Miss Cook!'

Caroline turned to Jack and shot him a cheeky wink.

❄

'Good game, good game!' cheered Brian, positively beaming at the pair of them.

'Only because you won,' laughed Caroline.

'My bad!' said Jack with a sheepish smile.

Caroline's stellar scores hadn't quite been man enough to bring their team average up enough to beat Brian – not when Jack fumbled with nearly every turn he took. It turned out Caroline was even more of a distraction when she was standing close enough that he could smell her perfume.

'I'd ask you guys for another game,' said Brian, 'but I think it's getting a bit too full in here to be safe!'

Sure enough, the minute they'd come to the end of their game, the no-man's land around the board had instantly started to fill up with festive revellers again.

'You're right. Plus, it's getting hot in here,' said Caroline, fanning her face.

'Fancy a breath of fresh air?' said Jack.

He still needed to tell her his news, but somehow, he didn't think the crowded bar of the Dolphin and Anchor was *quite* the place.

Caroline nodded, smiling up at him.

'Thanks for the game, Brian!' said Jack.

'Anytime,' said Brian, grinning at him as Trish sidled over. He wrapped an arm around her shoulders. 'I hope you hang around these parts long enough for a rematch!'

Jack was about to answer when he felt Caroline's fingers lace through his own and tug him towards the door. He just had long enough to register the look of delight on Trish's face before he found himself being pulled through the crowd by Caroline. They didn't stop until they were through the door and standing on the cobbled street.

'That's better!' sighed Caroline, dropping Jack's hand so that she could stretch her bare arms out wide. She sucked in a deep lungful of chilly air before letting it out in a long plume of foggy breath.

'You're going to freeze!' said Jack, rubbing his palms together.

'Hardly!' said Caroline, turning her flushed face towards him, her red dress sparkling under the Christmas lights. 'But if you feel cold, you could always put your Christmas tree bonnet back on.'

'Good call!' said Jack, and with a broad smile, he pulled the monstrosity back out of his pocket and pulled it onto his head, making Caroline giggle.

'There he is, ladies and gents,' Caroline announced to the empty street. 'Jack Jones – international heartthrob!'

'Oh… so you think I'm a heartthrob, huh?' said Jack, with a sly smile.

'There he goes again, fishing for compliments,' giggled Caroline, still playing up to an invisible crowd. 'So… were you hounded for your autograph the whole time you were carolling?'

'Hardly!' laughed Jack. 'Just a couple of times… and one of them was Milly's assistant.'

'Jo?' said Caroline.

'That's the one,' said Jack. 'I think she just wanted an excuse to ask me if the pair of us were seeing each other.'

Caroline snorted in amusement. 'And how did you get out of that one?'

'I told her… we hadn't got to that bit of the story yet,' said Jack, unable to take his eyes off her.

'You did, huh?' said Caroline. 'Smooth. What's that, a line from one of your films?'

'Nope,' said Jack, his voice going quiet. He took a step towards her and reached for her hand again. When she took it, he raised her fingers to his lips and kissed them before staring for a long moment at the yellow plastic ring. 'Just me… being hopeful.'

Caroline held his eye for a long moment before looking away to stare out across the velvet darkness of the marshes.

'So…' she said, 'when do you leave?'

'What, tonight?' said Jack.

Caroline shook her head, still not looking at him. 'For New Zealand, I mean. When do you start filming?'

'I don't,' said Jack.

Finally, it was time to tell her his news.

'You don't?' she said.

'I turned it down,' he said.

Caroline turned to him so quickly that he'd be surprised if she hadn't just cricked her neck.

'What? But why?!' she gasped, her eyes going wide.

'I… erm…'

Because of you. Because I like you.

'Because…' Jack took a deep breath. 'Because I like this story better… and I want to see where it goes.'

'Aww, what a line!' chuckled Caroline.

'What?' said Jack, starting to tug her towards him. 'Too wooden for you?'

'Nope,' she said, glancing up at his ridiculous hat as he looped his arms around her waist. Then she met his eye with a smile that rendered him completely speechless. 'Nope,' she said again. 'That was just about perfect! Hey – are you cold? You're shaking!'

Jack simply shook his head. Then he wrapped her a little tighter in his arms and bent to kiss Caroline Cook under Crumbleton's twinkling Christmas lights.

CHAPTER 17

CAROLINE

Caroline rolled over and yawned. Her eyes fluttered open, only to be greeted by silvery, early morning light. For a moment she was caught somewhere between the delicious dream she'd been having, and real life. In her dream, there had been carols and snowflakes, the sound of the sea and the most handsome dork-of-a-man she'd ever laid eyes on.

The distant sound of waves on a beach reached her ears, and a rush of tingling electricity ran through her from head to toe. Caroline grabbed the edges of the green and red festive duvet cover and tugged it up to her chin as she struggled to sit up.

The movement sent something tumbling off the pillows beside her. Reaching down, Caroline pulled out a little square package from the nest of bedding – along with a red envelope. It had already been torn open and emptied of its contents.

Turning it over, Caroline saw Jack's name in swirling golden letters. It was crossed out with two dark pencil lines, and underneath it was a scruffy scrawl.

Merry Christmas! Gone down to the beach for a dip. I'll be back to make you breakfast before you know it!
Just Jack x
P.S. Waking up next to you = best present ever!

'Soppy git,' she murmured, grinning down at the words as the perfect dream she'd been having merged with reality.

Because... it was all real.

After heading back inside the Dolphin and Anchor to continue celebrating with the rest of the town, it hadn't taken Jack long to realise that his ride back to Crumbleton Sands wasn't going to happen. Brian had got his wires crossed, thinking Jack had somewhere to stay in Crumbleton for the night, and had been indulging in the fortified mulled wine with abandon.

Caroline had been more than happy to swoop to the rescue, and the pair of them had held hands all the way back to her little flat. After demonstrating quite how tiny and cramped her sofa was – and the fact that it really wasn't a suitable spot for a Hollywood star to spend the night – Caroline had offered an alternative arrangement which was far more comfortable... even if it had produced a great deal of giggling.

On Christmas Eve morning, the pair of them had dashed around the town for some last-minute supplies. Then Caroline had driven Jack back to his beautiful seaside home... and simply never left.

'I can't believe I'm here for Christmas!' she whispered, still in shock about the fact that this was real rather than some delicious dream.

Jack's scruffy, motheaten sofa had been proved to be a far more comfortable spot than her own. The pair of them had spent most of the previous afternoon tangled together in its depths, laughing, sipping chocolate and kissing as the wood burner crackled merrily in the background. Caroline knew for a fact that she'd remember those hot chocolate-flavoured kisses for the rest of her life.

Giving a delighted wriggle in her festive PJs, Caroline turned her attention to the little wrapped present. Should she wait for Jack before she opened it? Surely not... considering he'd left it on his pillow for her?

With a shrug, Caroline promptly tore into the wrapping paper to reveal an ornate box. Light blue with a familiar monogram - the kind of box that came from a seriously posh jewellery shop. She swallowed nervously. Surely... surely it was a bit too soon for something like this?

With shaking fingers, Caroline popped open the lid... and let out a loud snort of laughter. Nestled on a bed of duck-egg blue velvet was an ugly, yellow plastic bracelet – complete with several glittering "diamonds". Next to it was a scrap of paper.

To go with your engagement ring!

Caroline promptly took it out of the box and pulled it onto her wrist. It was… perfect.

Scrambling from beneath the cosy covers, she hurried over to the window and pulled the curtains back. It was snowing again. Not a heavy flurry like the storm that had stranded her here in the first place – but soft, delicate flakes fluttering from a silvery sky.

Could there be a more beautiful sight to wake up to on Christmas morning?

Caroline's eyes drifted beyond the dunes to the sea. She could swear she could just make out two tiny dots of colour – a Santa hat and a swim float cutting through the chilly waves. She watched for a long moment… and then jumped into action.

Scuttling over to the foot of the bed, Caroline pulled her warm, fluff-lined boots onto her bare feet. Then she grabbed Jack's giant sweatshirt from the trail of clothes he'd discarded the previous night and pulled it right over the top of her pyjamas.

It was time to head down to the beach. After all – how often was she going to get to spend Christmas morning by the sea with a hunky Hollywood actor?

The thought made her heart sink. She didn't ever want this dream to end… and yet, even if Jack wasn't going to be filming in New Zealand, he was bound to leave for another job before too long, wasn't he?!

Shaking her head, Caroline put the thought to the back of her mind as she pelted down the stairs towards the front door. She was here now, and she was going to make the most of every second of this magical Christmas.

Cutting around the corner and hopping over the spot in the fence Jack had shown her the previous day, Caroline made her way across the dunes and onto the beach. As she approached the frothy shoreline where the gentle waves rushed in to greet her, Jack turned and started swimming in her direction.

Caroline wrapped her arms around herself, snuggling deeper into her pilfered sweatshirt and wishing she'd thought to grab a hat as the breeze swirled dancing snowflakes around her.

'Hey, Mr Film Star!' she called, as Jack hauled himself out of the sea and came dripping towards her in his wetsuit, Santa hat still perched on top of his head. 'Merry Christmas!'

'You too!' said Jack, grinning at her as he approached. 'Fancy seeing you here – but you didn't have to come down to freeze just because I'm an idiot.'

'It's not often I get to walk to the beach in my PJs on Christmas morning,' said Caroline.

'Yeah – I do see your point,' said Jack. 'Though I'm looking forward to making it a new tradition.'

'What, back in California?' said Caroline, doing her best to rein in a little pout and failing miserably.

Jack shook his head. 'Here. I'm staying put.'

'But, what about work?' said Caroline, hugging herself even tighter as Jack stood, dripping in front of her. 'Actually... come on – we can talk about this inside. Let's go before you freeze!'

Jack grabbed her hand and tugged her back towards him before she could take off. His eyes landed on her plastic bracelet and he grinned. 'My next job's in London.'

'You... wait...' spluttered Caroline. 'As in London... England?!'

'That's the one,' said Jack, grinning at her with slightly blue lips. 'Heard of it?'

'Might have,' said Caroline. 'But what...?'

'Remember the animation about the dog in space?' he said.

'The one you were reading because you were enjoying the story?' said Caroline.

'That's the one,' Jack nodded. 'Meet the new voice of Buster!'

'Oh wow... congratulations!' said Caroline. 'So you'll be living...?' she couldn't bring herself to finish the question.

'Here,' said Jack with a little nod as he started to shiver in earnest. 'If I can work out some kind of friendly agreement with the local press, that would be even better.'

'I'm sure we can come to some arrangement,' said Caroline. She was desperate to wrap her arms around him... but given that he was all salty, sandy and dripping...

'So,' said Jack, 'shall we say... same time, same place, next Christmas?'

Caroline grinned at him. 'Perfect,' she said, stepping forward and placing a gentle kiss on his lips. He tasted of salt water and cinnamon.

'Come on,' said Jack as she finally stepped back, 'you need a shower.'

'Wait, what?!' laughed Caroline. 'I think you'll find that's you!'

Jack shook his head, and with one swift movement, he scooped her off her feet. Caroline wrapped her arms around his neck just as water from his wetsuit started to seep into her pyjamas.

'Gross!' she squealed.

'Rude!' laughed Jack, snuggling her even closer to his chest. Caroline tugged at the pompom of his Santa hat in retaliation.

'Come on, Mr Film Star,' she giggled, 'put me down – it's time for that shower!'

'Yep it is,' said Jack, grinning at her, 'but there's no way I'm putting you down.' With that, he strode of up the beach through the swirling snowflakes, with Caroline in his arms.

EPILOGUE

CRUMBLETON TIMES AND ECHO - 28TH DECEMBER

Rookie Caroller Hits High Notes and Fundraising Goals in Christmas Cringe Headwear!

Congratulations to our beloved Crumbleton Carollers for raising a record amount of donations for the Museum Fund during last week's Christmas Lights event. No one's quite sure what made everyone so generous, but there's rumblings about it having something to do with our fresh face's festive hat! Get ready for next year, folks, I've got a feeling there's going to be some stiff competition as our crooners do their best to outdo each other with their Cringemas Crowns!

Celeb Sighting at the Christmas Lights!

It's not just the carollers who were turning heads at

this year's event. Huge thanks to one very special celebrity for their surprise appearance. That's right folks, I'm talking about our very own Ruby Hutchinson who managed to tear herself away from her laptop to support the event. Congratulations to our awesome author for finishing her most recent (soon-to-be) bestseller, and for dealing so graciously with one particularly loony fan who [allegedly!] tried to get her to sign his butt cheeks in the Dolphin and Anchor.

New Year's Darts at the Dolphin & Anchor, Wednesday 7.30pm

A note from Brian Singer. If you'd like to join him for the New Year's Day darts game, there's a waiting list. He's currently got the board booked from midday until midnight.

A very Happy New Year to you all,
Caroline Cook, Editor.

THE END

ALSO BY BETH RAIN

Seabury Series:

Welcome to Seabury (Seabury Book 1)

Trouble in Seabury (Seabury Book 2)

Christmas in Seabury (Seabury Book 3)

Sandwiches in Seabury (Seabury Book 4)

Secrets in Seabury (Seabury Book 5)

Surprises in Seabury (Seabury Book 6)

Dreams and Ice Creams in Seabury (Seabury Book 7)

Mistakes and Heartbreaks in Seabury (Seabury Book 8)

Laughter and Happy Ever After in Seabury (Seabury Book 9)

A Quiet Life in Seabury (Seabury Book 10)

In A Spin in Seabury (Seabury Book 11)

Living The Dream in Seabury (Seabury Book 12)

A Big Day in Seabury (Seabury Book 13)

Something Borrowed in Seabury (Seabury Book 14)

A Match Made in Seabury (Seabury Book 15)

Seabury Series Collections:

Kate's Story: Books 1 - 3

Hattie's Story: Books 4 - 6

Standalones: Books 7 - 9

Lizzie's Story: Books 10 - 12

Upper Bamton Series:

Upper Bamton: The Complete Series Collection: Books 1 - 4

Individual titles:

A New Arrival in Upper Bamton (Upper Bamton Book 1)

Rainy Days in Upper Bamton (Upper Bamton Book 2)

Hidden Treasures in Upper Bamton (Upper Bamton Book 3)

Time Flies By in Upper Bamton (Upper Bamton Book 4)

Standalone Books:

How to be Angry at Christmas

Crumbleton Series:

Coming Home to Crumbleton (Crumbleton Book 1)

Flowers Go Flying in Crumbleton (Crumbleton Book 2)

Match Point in Crumbleton (Crumbleton Book 3)

A Very Crumbleton Christmas (Crumbleton Book 4)

Little Bamton Series:

Little Bamton: The Complete Series Collection: Books 1 - 5

Individual titles:

Christmas Lights and Snowball Fights (Little Bamton Book 1)

Spring Flowers and April Showers (Little Bamton Book 2)

Summer Nights and Pillow Fights (Little Bamton Book 3)

Autumn Cuddles and Muddy Puddles (Little Bamton Book 4)

Christmas Flings and Wedding Rings (Little Bamton Book 5)

Crumcarey Island Series:

Crumcarey Island Series Collection: Books 1 - 5

Individual titles:

Christmas on Crumcarey (Crumcarey Island Book 1)

All Change on Crumcarey (Crumcarey Island Book 2)

Making Waves on Crumcarey (Crumcarey Island Book 3)

Fool's Gold on Crumcarey (Crumcarey Island Book 4)

A Fresh Start on Crumcarey (Crumcarey Island Book 5)

WRITING AS BEA FOX

What's a Girl To Do? The Complete Series

Individual titles:

The Holiday: What's a Girl To Do? (Book 1)

The Wedding: What's a Girl To Do? (Book 2)

The Lookalike: What's a Girl To Do? (Book 3)

The Reunion: What's a Girl To Do? (Book 4)

At Christmas: What's a Girl To Do? (Book 5)

ABOUT THE AUTHOR

Beth Rain has always wanted to be a writer and has been penning adventures for characters ever since she learned to stare into the middle-distance and daydream.

She recently moved to a windswept, Scottish island, and it is a dream come true to spend her days hanging out with Bob – her trusty laptop – scoffing crisps and chocolate while dreaming up swoony love stories for all her imaginary friends.

Beth's writing will always deliver on the happy-ever-afters, so if you need cosy… you're in safe hands!

Visit www.bethrain.com for all the bookish goodness and keep up with all Beth's news by joining her newsletter!

facebook.com/BethRainBooks
twitter.com/bethrainauthor
instagram.com/bethrainauthor

Printed in Great Britain
by Amazon